MW00979965

Giver of Gifts

By Terry Persun

A Palmland Publishing Product

Cover Art-Rocket Digital

About author Terry L. Persun

Terry Persun has won several awards for his 2003 release, Wolf's Rite, including the Star of Washington Award and the POW First Place Award for best fiction. Wolf's Rite was also a finalist in the ForeWord Magazine Book of the Year Award. Terry's first novel, The Witness Tree, was mentioned as a hand-selling favorite in Publishers Weekly, and received positive reviews from Today's Librarian and other important trade magazines. Terry has appeared on television, been interviewed on numerous radio stations across the country. His novels have been reviewed in dozens of newspapers and magazines. Giver of Gifts is his third published work of adult fiction.

Other Works by Terry Persun

Novels:

Wolf's Rite
(Russell Dean & Company)
(Palmland Publishing)

The Witness Tree
(Implosion Press)
(Russell Dean & Company)
(Palmland Publishing)

Poetry:

Barn Tarot
(Implosion Press)
(Palmland Publishing)

Poetry Chapbooks:

In the Story
Three Lives
Plant-Animal-I
Hollow Good-Byes
Dandelion Soul
Behind a Red Gate

Giver of Gifts

A novel by:
Terry L. Persun

All rights reserved. No part of this book, form or substance, maybe reproduced or transmitted in any form or by any means, electronic or mechanical, including but not limited to photocopying, recording, computer assisted data capture, or by any information storage and retrieval system without the prior written permission of the author. No adaptation of the material in this book may be used for stage, television, film, radio, or any other performance form, unless written authorization is obtained from the author.

All characters in this book are fictional. Similarities between characters and real individuals, living and dead, is coincidental.

Copyright © 2006
By Terry L. Persun

First printing Spring, 2006

ISBN# 1-933678-10-0

LIBRARY OF CONGRESS CATALOGING-IN-PUBLICATION DATA
Persun, Terry L.
     Giver of Gifts: a novel
        By / Terry L. Persun – First edition
     ISBN# 1-933678-10-0 (soft cover edition)
     1. Fiction, novel – United States, Pineland, FL   I. Title
     2. Mainstream, literary

Library of Congress Catalog Card Number   2006901647

 A Palmland Publishing Product

Acknowledgements

My gratitude goes first to Robert Fulton of RiverGeezer Editing for his initial editing of this novella. Thanks, also, to Jerani Queen for her proofreading skills. Further acknowledgment goes next to Lynn Park, the editor who honed this story into a fine piece of writing. And finally, I thank my dear, sweet wife, Catherine, for her continuous belief in me and my ability to create.

Giver of Gifts

a novel by

Terry Persun

edited by
Robert W. Fulton

© Spring, 2006

Adult Mainstream Fiction

All characters in this book are fictional.   Similarities between characters and real individuals, living and dead, are coincidental.

Chapter 1

Everything looked different now. That included the side hill, the snow, the fallen fence, the weeds, and the husk of the farmhouse. Jim ran his gloved hand along the window frame from top to bottom and let the paint peel and fall. A small breeze rounded the corner of the house and blew the chips across the porch. Then the air fell quiet again. The deer must have hidden well. Jim seldom bothered to load his rifle anymore, and always felt bad for the buck when Ed or Mel got lucky.

The wind picked up and whistled through the window. Spider webs, torn curtains, and frayed cloth from an abandoned sofa fluttered as Jim's eyes adjusted to the dark interior. He tucked his head deeper into the neck of his coat to keep warm. He leaned his rifle against the window frame and pushed the glass and dirt from the lip. With some difficulty, he stepped over the high sill and lowered his head to get in through the broken window. Everything lay dusty, drenched in shadow and unused. The stair railing toppled over at the bottom. A chandelier tipped slightly, hanging from frayed wires. He first looked around the living room. There were the tattered sofa and two side chairs. *One for him and one for her.* Hers was more delicate. His was worn through at the armrests. A broken lamp lay on a desk against the wall. Jim tried the drawers— all empty. The children, or the beneficiaries if children weren't in the picture, would have emptied the drawers. That thought saddened him. No children. Why, a farm needed children, if not to carry on after the parents were gone, then to liven the air with laughter. Jim thought how the children had brought happiness into his and Becky's home, until Connie died. Since that time, even Brad had become more serious about his life and more protective of his own wife.

Closer to the stairs, Jim found evidence of nests. Squirrel, rat, raccoon—he had no idea, but something had been piling stuffing from the furniture, mixing it with leaves, grass, and dust balls. The first set of stairs led to a landing, a turn, and more stairs. Jim tested every other step, steadying himself with one hand against the wall. At the landing, he unzipped his coat halfway. The still air of the stairwell felt warm despite the broken window downstairs. A thick, sweet odor hung in the air. Ahead of him another broken window, a crust of sparkling white all the way across the sill where the snow, warmed from the sun, had frozen through the night.

Jim explored two of the bedrooms quickly, but felt a rush of anxiety, a sense of intrusion, when he stepped into the master bedroom. Two lives, he thought, two bodies had lived, loved, and died beneath a hand-embroidered quilt that still lay across the bed. Couldn't the children bear to remove it? Couldn't anyone? Were the farmer and his wife in love or merely in commitment? He decided, because of the quilt alone, that they had been lovers, deep, passionate lovers. Jim touched the quilt and it felt warm, even through his glove. He jerked his hand away.

He had always wanted to explore the place, and now he had. Maybe he'd come back, go inside the barn. He could do anything now that he was dying, would die. The thought notched a feeling of resolve into him. He could handle death, even his own. It was life he had had problems with. But now, even his life was all right.

After he climbed back out of the window, Jim picked up the rifle he'd left on the porch. He would follow the stone fence into the north field, then enter the woods, and make his way around the mountain back to the hunting cabin.

It was a brilliant day. The sun perched above the trees and spread a warm glow along the side of the hill, pushing shadows mixed with patched of brilliance deep into the woods. The cold wind off the snow became less biting along the length of the fence, which shielded Jim from the wind's full force. He heard snow clumps drop from trees, as the wind passed through. The woods were dense with snow, although the snow in the clearings and the expanse of field he walked through had melted down to form a thin crust that sparkled in the sun just like the snow on the second-story window ledge.

Jim climbed over the fence, careful not to topple any of the stones, and headed into the woods along the back of the hill. The walk around would give him time to think. He was hungry. He could already sense the warmth of the fire against his face.

A short distance into the woods, Jim heard two shots go off and felt pain run through his body. "Please don't let it be," he said, looking upward into the tops of the pines. He waited, but heard no other shots. He threw his rifle over his shoulder like an unnecessary walking stick. He sometimes wondered why he still bothered to carry the thing. Tradition? Habit? So other hunters wouldn't think he was nuts? He had never shot a deer, even in his younger years. Small game, yes. But deer? He'd seen them, just never lifted his rifle, never got a bead on them. Several times he'd shooed them away. "Well, hello there, deer. You really shouldn't be out in these woods today. Lucky you happened onto me." He was not against hunting; he just didn't shoot deer.

His mind wandered over those days while he crunched through the top crust of snow. It amused him to think about the past that way. He had always been the quiet type, often very passive. Rebecca berated him about it in the beginning. She wished for a more aggressive husband, one who fought for a better life, more money, more power. Eventually she saw that he could never make himself fit into a corporate mold. He loved his job teaching junior high school English. He looked forward to the summers off where he would pick up a different part-time job each year. Labor-intensive, mindless work that rested him for the new school year.

Going through the woods around the hill, Jim had the choice to think abstractly or to focus on the moment at hand. He drew himself into the neck of his jacket whenever the wind rushed overhead. It kept him warm and also protected him from falling snow that might slip down inside his coat. The smells and sounds of the woods were unique every season, but Jim loved winter best, with its muffled tones and crisp, clean air, the slight scent of pine.

On the last leg of his slow progression, Jim followed what looked like a path although there were no tracks in the snow. The underbrush had been parted; whether by man's technical hand or beasts' use over and over didn't matter. The path was set and he planned to explore it. The path continued to open up and reveal more as he walked deeper into the woods. The incline was slight, but he knew he headed uphill.

As the woods got denser, the path became more apparent, yet there were still no prints to give away what, or who, kept the path cleared. As the ground leveled off, the wind picked up. He wasn't at the top of the hill, but somewhere near it. He continued following the path, turning one way then another. He was almost sure it was a hikers' trail, or a horseback trail for some local 4-H club. As he walked on, he became more winded, his heartbeat unusually fast. He knew he wasn't out of shape. Yet the combination of shortness of breath and increased heartbeat was even more confusing when he considered how invigorated he felt. Around another turn and Jim fell into a run, his heart pumping, his breath heavy. Holding the stock of the rifle in his right hand, the weapon swung next to him like a relay race baton. He got warm and unzipped his jacket completely.

As he wound through the woods, first going along level ground, then uphill again, and finally, in a spiral, into a steep decline, Jim could feel the lump under his arm rubbing as his arms rocked forward and back. Life was finite, at least physical life was. He stopped jogging and leaned against a tree. He lifted the rifle into the air and placed his left hand under his right arm and pressed. "Damn," he said. "I'm a dead man." He breathed deeply and spit into the snow. He let his arms fall next to his sides. His right hand gripped the rifle—the weapon, cold and black, that killed living things. Life was much too precious at that moment to ever want to use the rifle.

The trail came to a fork and Jim contemplated going back the way he came. He felt excited, jittery, like he had overdosed on his prescription. He didn't know if he wanted to continue into the woods or not. *A little ways more*, he thought, *only a little farther*. There was a good chance that the trail circled back onto itself, anyway.

He thought of leaving the rifle. He no longer needed it. But Brad would want it. Jim's grandfather, father, and now he had used it. The stock of the 44-40 he carried was cold.

Jim zipped up his jacket halfway. The breeze that worked its way down from the tops of the trees touched his face with gentle hands, and he raised his face toward it, accepting it.

Farther down the path, his mind slipped into thoughts about Connie when she was a little girl. He stopped the tears before they got out. It had been a long time since he thought about her as a young girl. He tried to get his mind to focus on the woods and the path, to separate himself from the pain born of memories of someone he would soon join.

The snow appeared to be deeper. Dense clumps hung over the tree branches and perched on top of the thicker, stronger bushes. Even the sky overhead took on a deeper hue. Jim looked down. His eyes widened and his breath quickened—hoof prints. Everywhere. When did they start? He looked around. They came from all angles, from both directions on the path, from the woods on either side of him. Fresh tracks, but there were no deer. He bent down. It was almost scary that he could be so mindless. Could he have stumbled into a herd and not even noticed? He stood up and proceeded down the path. Beyond a small grove of pine trees, there looked to be a clearing. He headed for it. When he stepped around the trees, he saw them. Deer. One lying down and two standing. Two does and a buck. Jim stopped dead in his tracks. The deer didn't move. They weren't threatening at all.

For a long time Jim stood still, staring at the three deer, which stared back at him. There were hoof prints everywhere, as though thirty invisible deer were standing there. The air filled with what appeared to be the golden glow of dusk, but different as well. Perhaps these new variations in color entered from overhead. Perhaps they were from the deeper colors in the sky, the depth of green from the trees, or some odd ricochet of light off the snow. All Jim knew was that the deer looked unnatural. Fantasy deer. Mannequins. Their only movement was an occasional twitch of the ears. Green, blue, and brown converged, part deer, part light, and waltzed as the trees swayed in the wind.

Jim suddenly became cold, particularly his right hand, the one holding the rifle. Once stabilized and calm, he braved movement, first by bending at the waist and lowering the rifle onto the snow. Then he zipped his jacket to the neck; a small string of goosebumps formed and ran down his spine and over his shoulders. His face felt hot. His mind raced to the old house and incorporated its dark, shadowy spaces downstairs and the loving spaces in the master bedroom into his now growing emotional attachment to this moment, to the deer, the woods, the odd light, and himself. Together, there were emotional and physical energies he couldn't understand, could hardly fathom except that he knew each aspect intimately, having experienced it.

He took a step forward expecting everything before him to disintegrate and for the face of some fat nurse to be staring down at him, lifting the cold white sheet over his face. But to his complete surprise, nothing of the kind happened. His heart raced faster and he felt he could hardly contain the energy. His body wanted to run. *No, be cautious.* The six-point buck stepped out from behind the supine doe; the other doe, standing near the buck, turned her head to watch him move. Just from watching him, Jim could feel the power of the male. His smooth motions were like an ice skater's, not an animal's. Jim knew that movement was what animals were all about: migratory, life-securing, pleasurable movement.

The buck walked slowly, as if concerned that it would scare Jim away. And Jim considered stepping back to his original position and reaching for his rifle. The odd light ran across the deer's back, the wind rustled the trees, the woods closed in and held them all there in that place. Jim became part of the deer and the grove and the strange world of light and wind. Even his death was a part of this place that seemed to create itself out of, and around, him and his experiences. How oddly everything here belonged to him and he belonged to it. His love and anger and euphoria and pain— inside and outside him.

Jim waited for the male to come closer. Its brown eyes glistened and its nose dripped. A peculiar, yet authentic, smell emanated from the animal. Jim lifted his hand the way one human does to another human.

The buck's head dropped to a curious nose-out position. It continued to step closer; the wide breast and heavy haunches floated towards him. The sound of crunching snow verified that some kind of physical reality still existed. Never before had Jim experienced, or heard of anyone else experiencing, such a strange encounter with wild animals. He wondered if somehow several deer from some nearby petting zoo had escaped. That would explain their fearlessness.

With that thought still struggling inside Jim's mind, the buck lifted its head and looked into Jim's eyes. Jim heard the words, "No, that is not it." He stepped backward in a reverse run and tripped through the snow, landing on his back. The rifle lay near his hand, but he didn't grab it. He only looked at its long black barrel lying in the snow next to him.

"Do not be afraid." The words came from the direction of the deer. The syllables entered his ears as though they had passed lips and rode the wind over to him. Yet the deer's lips had not moved.

Jim stayed on his back, lifted his head, and waited for more words. He couldn't speak. There was nothing to say. In a moment, the buck came over to him, not in curiosity, but in determination and confidence.

"Fear does not become you. Abandon it."

It was an order Jim didn't know how to respond to. He reached for the rifle, but when his hand met cold steel, he didn't grasp it. Instead he rolled to his side and sat up. "What do you want from me?"

The buck turned its neck and looked back in an expression of concern for the other deer, a way to include them, to see if they heard the question. The standing doe shifted her feet and perked up her ears. The other doe lowered her head, nose out, brown eyes wide. The buck turned back around to Jim. "We want nothing."

"Then . . . "

"We are the gift—" the standing doe said.

"—and you are the giver," the other doe completed her statement.

"But if you're the gift, I can't be the giver," Jim said.

"Without you, we cannot be what we are," the standing doe replied.

It was too confusing for him. Something didn't fit properly. *It wasn't a gift, it was a miracle.* There was no other word. Either he had died, gone crazy, or it was a miracle. He didn't feel dead or crazy; that left only one explanation. What else could it be?

The buck's ears twitched expressively, then the first doe's ears did the same. *They must be communicating among themselves.* Jim stood up from the snow and picked up the rifle. There was no longer any sense of threat from either side. Miracles were like that, he thought. He followed the buck to where the doe were.

As though invited to do so, Jim knelt behind the doe that was lying down and placed his gloved hand on her bony neck. He held the rifle upright. *It would make such an odd picture,* he thought.

The light around them remained peculiar. Time slowed, even though his heart raced. "I want to understand," he said to them. "Why are you here? What gift do you bring? What am I giving?"

The doe in front of him spoke. The words took hold of his ears and mind at once. Even his body felt them. "Your being is a part, a calling. We were chosen as the gift."

"Then how am I the giver?"

She rose from the ground then, and turned to him. Jim rose also, the rifle in his right hand not a weapon, but an article of clothing he wore into the woods.

"You give."

"But I'm receiving the gift."

The buck put his nose to Jim's elbow and nudged him.

Jim raised his face to a soft wind blowing into the small clearing. The snow shifted like a light fog over the ground and tree branches; some clumps hit the ground with muffled thuds. He felt oversensitive. His face, his nose, his body. All the smells and the color, everywhere. If the deer were a gift then so was this place. How had he given it to himself? Why had he? It was beautiful and sad. What could he do with this gift to himself, but know that it happened only to him? Why had he complicated his life with a miracle? He looked around, held out his arms, and dropped the rifle. He became a human cross; trying to grasp the universe, trying to feel everything around him, take it all inside.

Twilight fell around them. The forest remained quiet, only the sound of wind, small birds, and squirrels. "I want to know more. Don't let me forget this. Please, I want to go back with every memory." He was afraid of forgetting details, because there were no details. The closer to night it became, the less he seemed to know or be able to grasp.

As darkness settled around them, Jim realized that he must go. Once he left, he knew the miracle would be over. "One more thing," he said. "How can I be sure this happened, that this was what it was?" He looked to each of them. "I need one more sign, one more." He knew he was being unreasonable. A sign to prove a miracle? How human not to believe his own eyes and ears and heart. "Please," he said, "then I'll go."

Then, all around, in each set of footsteps in the snow, amidst the dancing light of near darkness, color and sound fell into flesh and bone like falling stars fall into the ocean. Deer appeared around him, fading into view one behind another as though they had been there all the time, but hidden from his eyes behind the very light that now seemed to bring them into view. Jim stood in silence.

"Remember that you are a part of everything, forever," the buck said.

"Now go," they said.

And the forest shook itself awake. Jim left.

Chapter 2

The voices faded behind Jim. The moon rose above tree level and cleared a path. Light off the snow guided him to the side of the hill. Echoes pushed him forward. Images of what had happened sustained him in the cold of night. He tried to grasp everything that had happened, their words and his sensations, but became less sure of the specifics as he mulled them over. He knew—or hoped—that things would come to him as time went on. That the details of the event would surface like small lifeboats in a sea of survivors. He had been crying. He could feel the dried tears on his face. Part of him wanted to believe that it had been just a dream, but inside he knew it had all been real.

Darkness fell evenly across the fields and forest. The moon on the snow kept it light enough for him to find his way back.

When he approached the small cabin, Ed and Mel rushed from the door. "What took you?" Mel said as matter-of-factly as he could muster.

"You won't believe it," Jim said. Yet, even at that moment, he debated with himself how much to tell them. He knew they wouldn't believe him. But they were his friends, and since there was an explanation they should hear it.

The two men gathered around him, concerned and relieved at once. The cabin door stood open. A dim light fell onto the small porch and out into the cold night. Through the door, the flickering of firelight could be seen, but not the fire. The smell of smoke was in the air.

Jim handed over his rifle.

"We thought you were face down somewhere," Ed said.

"What'd you do, take a nap?" Mel added. "We looked and called. Didn't you hear us?"

"I couldn't hear anything. My mind was too caught up in it all," Jim said.

"In what? Hunting?" Mel asked.

"No. A miracle."

Ed and Mel looked at each other as they ushered Jim into the cabin. The warm air fell over them like a heavy quilt. Jim hadn't noticed before, but his heart rate had dropped to normal. "I need rest," he said, taking off his coat.

"What about this miracle thing?" Mel asked.

"I don't know if I should talk about it right now."

"Why's that?" Mel couldn't let it go.

Jim, with Ed and Mel close behind, entered the single bedroom where there were two beds and a cot. Past years, Jim got the cot, but this year, Ed took it. Jim knew that the way they treated him now was a reflection on his condition, but he tended not to be too assertive, so he let them, though it wasn't necessary. He liked the feelings of roughing it he got when he slept on the cot. This trip he had given up that sensation so that Ed and Mel could feel better. "I'm sleeping here tonight." Jim flopped onto the cot, still fully dressed.

Ed and Mel said, "No," at the same time, then looked at each other.

"I love this old cot. I miss it." Jim put his hands behind his head and closed his eyes. He heard his friends shuffling around and whispering.

"Jim?" Mel said.

"Yeah?"

"What happened out there?"

Without opening his eyes, Jim said, "Something magnificent." The last image he saw flashed through his mind— all the deer appearing, once again. "Something magical." He opened his eyes and turned his head. Ed and Mel sat on their beds looking at him. Jim couldn't tell if they stared in interest or in concern. "You won't believe me, I tell you. You'll just think I'm nuts."

"No, we won't," Mel looked at Ed for confirmation and Ed obediently shook his head.

Jim propped himself on one elbow. His eyes felt extremely heavy. "If I told you, point-blank, that I saw a flying saucer and little aliens, would you believe me?"

Ed sat up straight. Again, the two friends looked over at one another.

"Did you?" Mel asked.

"No?" Ed said.

Jim had his answer, turned onto his back, and closed his eyes.

"He didn't mean that," Mel said.

"Really, I didn't, Jim," Ed said. "You know that. We've been friends too long. I didn't want to believe about the cancer"—that word he said in almost a whisper—"either, at first. Remember?"

Jim did remember. Ed had been there for as far back as Jim could go, from playgrounds and preschools, from girls and puppy love, and from secrets and indiscretions, all the way from childhood into the adult years. They had met up with Mel in high school. But Mel had come along well, and could be trusted.

"I don't know," Jim said, his tiredness slowing his words. He breathed deeper. His eyelids were too heavy to hold open. Maybe after a good rest, he'd be more coherent. "Tomorrow," he whispered. Just before falling off completely, Jim heard the concerned voices of the other two as they left the room. The conversation got farther and farther away until they were somewhere deep in the forest.

Jim slept in his clothes, a sound, heavy sleep. He remembered dreaming, but couldn't get a fix on what he dreamed. The first thing he did when he woke up was to reach under his arm. The lump always felt larger in the morning and Jim couldn't decide whether it really was larger or it just seemed that way. Ed and Mel were still asleep, so Jim tiptoed into the main room.

When he got out of the shower, he noticed that the clock over the stove read three o'clock. He remembered hitting the sack early the night before. Ed and Mel wouldn't be getting up for another two or three hours, so Jim made coffee. The fire had died out.

As he began to awaken, Jim went over his excursion step by step. He scratched his face and brushed his hair back. After drinking more coffee, he leaned his face into his hands, his elbows on the table. The three deer appeared before his tight-shut eyes. Their lips did not move, but their voices rang into him like an old church bell. "We are the gift. You are the giver." They had said other things, but this phrase stuck in his mind. He repeated it to himself, trying to let it sink in, trying to figure it out.

He thought back. He remembered kneeling there in the woods after the conversation with the deer. He had felt stronger then than he'd felt in months. So much stronger, in fact, that he had almost rejected his own determined decision to forgo treatment.

At one time, he had decided to have the lump removed— extract the nucleus of the cancer only. He didn't want to go through chemotherapy, or radiation treatments. Yet, there in the woods, his decision had begun to weaken. Where he had once resolved himself to death, now he wasn't so sure.

"You all right?" Ed stood near the table. He was showered and dressed.

Jim jumped.

"Sorry if I scared you."

"I was just thinking about . . . "

"Yesterday," Ed said. "We looked for you for hours."

"I was down by the old farm for a little while, but nowhere else."

"You should have heard us yelling for you." Ed poured himself coffee. He rubbed Jim's shoulder with his empty hand, then sat down next to him. "We've been friends a long time. You can tell me."

"It's difficult. I'm not always sure of everything. It's like the shifting shadows a car's headlights make when they run across your bedroom wall. You know what I mean? You remember the pattern, but you couldn't draw it on paper even if you had to. So, I don't know what to say, or even if I should say anything."

"You don't have to, Buddy." Ed rose, took Jim's coffee cup, and refilled it. "Why don't you try to tell me? Maybe it'll help you to remember."

Jim could hear an anxious twist escape through Ed's calm words.

Ed sat back down and placed Jim's cup in front of him. "Start anywhere you like. It doesn't have to be from the beginning."

"I met up with three deer." Jim felt silly already. It wasn't as though the deer were people.

"That's good." Ed was thinking hunting. "Did you load your rifle?"

"No, I mean . . . "

"I don't know why you even carry that thing anymore. It's been—"

"The deer talked," Jim blurted through Ed's comment.

"Well, uh, so . . . "

"I know you probably think I'm nuts. Maybe I am. Shit, I don't know what."

Ed tried to contain himself, but was having obvious problems. "You, uh, well . . ."

"Don't." Jim held up his hand to stop Ed before the conversation ended with Jim feeling completely mistrusted. "I can't explain anything. I can only tell you what happened, what I saw and what I heard. Their lips didn't even move."

"Then how'd they talk?" Ed leaned back in his chair.

Jim wondered if Ed had just told himself that it was all a dream and therefore removed reality from the situation. There was such a change in his demeanor. "They spoke in words…in my head." The statement sounded false even to Jim's own ears.

"What'd they say?"

"That they are the gift and that I am the giver."

"That's what they said?"

"'We are the gift. You are the giver.' Yes."

"Sounds like some Zen thing out of a book. What's it mean?"

"I don't know exactly."

"Well, I'll say this for those deer: they know you."

"How so?"

"You're a giver. Always have been."

"That's nice of you to say."

"Becky'll tell you too, I bet. So would your kids."

"Kids?"

"I mean, so would Brad."

"No, that's okay. Connie's only dead, not gone."

Ed smiled. "Any other details you can remember?"

"Some. The way my heart raced, how I breathed more rapidly, but never felt the least bit tired. The path."

"There's a path?"

"There was."

"I guess I thought you followed tracks when you said deer."

"There were no tracks. Until I got to this small clearing, then, suddenly, there were a lot of tracks. Everywhere. Out of nowhere." Jim decided against bringing up the other deer. He'd gone as far as he could, maybe too far.

"Maybe we could go there, if there's still a path. I'd like to see this place," Ed said.

"Maybe I'll go. Today. Alone," Jim said.

"I won't be a bother."

"No, I just think that it's gone. If there's any chance at all of them still being there, or the clearing being there"—Jim remembered the strangeness of the light, the complete otherworldliness of the place—"it'll be open only to me. Even at that I doubt it'll happen again."

"You think?" Ed was back to doubting.

Jim could imagine Ed thinking that if it couldn't be returned to, it couldn't have been there in the first place.

"I'm sorry. It's hard to believe." Jim drank half his coffee. "I'm going to try though. Alone."

"If that's what you want, then fine." Ed slapped the table with his palm. Then he patted Jim's forearm. "Anything else you want to say?"

Jim looked up and started to cry, not much, just slow tears. "You don't have to be nice. I don't know if I'd believe me. It's all right."

"You've never lied to me. Not in my whole life." Ed stood and rubbed Jim's shoulders. "The last few years have been rough. But I'm right here for you, Buddy. So is Mel."

Jim stood up quickly, pushing Ed away from him. "The deer talked. Don't placate me. I'm sick, but I'm not crazy. The cancer's not eating my brain away. It's eating the rest of me." Jim went to the closet and pulled out his coat and another sweatshirt. He put on his boots.

"Where you going this early in the morning? I believe you."

"It doesn't matter," Jim said.

"Sure it does, or you wouldn't be mad. You wouldn't be going out in the dark. Alone."

"I was alone yesterday. I've walked alone through these woods for years. I know that hill like the back of my hand."

Ed stepped forward while Jim readied himself for the cold. "Well, so do we, Jim, and we were all over that hill yesterday, and you weren't there."

There's the horned head of doubt Jim had expected. Nonetheless, he had been there. Somehow the clearing was there and wasn't there. "I told you, it was strange. I don't even understand it. Maybe Connie will believe me. I'll talk with her."

"Good God, don't start that again."

"I still talk to her, even if she doesn't talk back. I only let others off the hook, so they wouldn't have to feel sorry for me anymore."

"We never felt sorry for you."

"It doesn't matter. This is my fantasy, let me live it."

"There, you called it a fantasy." Ed looked satisfied.

Jim walked past him and out the door, but before closing it, he looked straight at Ed. "It's the truth. Can you live with that?"

He was outside again. It was still dark except for the blue glow from the snow-covered ground. Jim walked straight for the woods, which ran along the base of the hill and up its sides. With a gloved hand, he touched each tree as he passed. He was still there, still alive. The snow crunched under his feet. The slight wind tightened and froze his face so that he didn't want to move his mouth for fear it would crack. Licking his lips, he expected ice to form over them. How quickly they dried. After a while, he turned to walk down, around the hill, near the stone fence. Opposite the old farmhouse, Jim found a tree overlooking the property. He brushed some snow off the ground with his hands and sat down. Although the ground was cold, Jim soon fell into a comfort he had not known for years. He was completely alone. The only sound was a soft wind through the trees. Nothing moved.

The farmhouse stood black against the snow and the dark sky. A slight cloud cover held back most of the starlight. The snow lay like a giant shadow over the field, darkened only by the real shadows of trees near the perimeter.

Jim leaned against the tree and felt the warmth of its life penetrate him, even in such a bitter cold. He let his mind wander along the fence and field. He remembered the farmhouse and the untouched master bedroom, and thought about his own strained marriage to Becky. Had he known he would bring such pain into her life, with the death of Connie and now his own, he never would have married her. Were the small joys she had experienced worth all this pain? Jim rubbed his temples to relieve the pressure. His gloves felt rough so he removed them. At first, his hot fingers felt good on his face, then they too cooled and he put his gloves back on.

He waited patiently for the sun to rise and bring new warmth to the day. He decided to retrace his steps the best he could, starting with the farmhouse.

When the sun first appeared, it was a glow around the treetops. Its rays penetrated the clouds like headlights in the fog. The farmhouse—he wondered if the farmer and his wife ever viewed their own home in early morning from the angle at which he sat— lit up with a soft, morning brilliance. The window at the top of the stairs stayed black except for the frame, which reflected a smooth white. The lip of the sill still held its sparkling snow buildup. From a distance, it was difficult to realize that the house was abandoned, except for the frayed curtain flapping in the wind through the kitchen window.

The barn leaned to one side. It must have been ignored for years even before the farmer and his wife died. Had they died together? In that bed? Jim hoped so, for the sake of romance. It must have broken the farmer's heart to see his barn go unused. Jim could imagine how he would have felt, taking walks around and through it, the total frustration of being unable to do anything about it.

When the sun rose enough to light the field in front of the house, Jim rose too, and headed for the farm. This time he planned to explore the barn first.

He climbed over the stone fence and welcomed the sun's warmth. The clouds had released their grip on the starlight. The snow glistened like diamonds and crunched like small stones under his feet. He felt invigorated, striding straight for the barn. Halfway there, he heard two shots then three more, and paused to say a silent prayer for the deer.

When he reached the barn, he squeezed through the partially open doors in the front, and stepped headlong into the psychedelic speckled light of the sun penetrating through slits in the roof. Some of the bins still held bales of old hay. An area had been set aside as pigpens, equipped with slop troughs along one side. Old tractor parts, including tires, seats, and what appeared to be the remains of an engine, lay in the back, but the rest of the tractor was gone. A manure spreader sat alone off to one side. The boards on its bottom and sides were warped and broken.

Looking around, Jim calculated what it would take to repair

the barn. Most of the work would be labor-intensive cleaning and organizing. That was except for the barn's obvious lean to the north, which would require replacing some pretty expensive structural beams. He'd spring for the cost of steel I-beams, if it were his to rebuild.

Jim ran his hand along everything that came within reach as he explored the hay bins and feeding pens. The patches of light and dark along the walls, floor, and roof stimulated his mind in strange ways. He wanted to lose himself, forget his own problems, and just feel. Lately, he had spent a lot of time with his physical sensations: looking, smelling, and touching everything. Sometimes at school, he'd just stare at the kids sitting with their heads down, working on their quizzes. Life had become more important now that there was a definite end to it. He almost looked forward to the pain of death itself as another, his last, sensual experience to explore. Becky didn't feel the same at all when he told her how he felt, but then, she had in her mind, he was sure, an indefinite lifespan. She wasn't dying.

The barn had kept his own death separated from him for a short while, as he got caught up in daydreams of repairs and of its possible past appearance and usefulness. Just like the time before Connie's death still existed for him, the past of the barn was still there to explore. All he had to do was allow it to come through. There was nothing like exploring and daydreaming to forget problems, but eventually reality always turns dreams back into the ether they are. While bending to pick up an old wooden pitchfork, Jim felt his coat push into the lump under his arm.

He sat down on a dust-covered potato crate. "Good God." *Connie, help me figure all this out.*

There was no reply, only the relative silence of an old barn being pushed and twisted by the wind, being exhaled and inhaled.

Occasionally Jim noticed as dust or snow, excited by the wind, brushed across the barn floor or fell from the rafters. He waited for the answer he knew would not come. *If I'm the gift giver, why didn't I give myself life? Or some kind of answer?*

The situation reminded him of how his students always wanted a definitive answer, how frustrated they got having to figure things out on their own. Now he had placed himself in a similar situation. But if it was true that he only needed to figure things out on his own, then it meant that there was an answer. Perhaps the meaning of the deer's words was as simple as what Ed had told him, that he had always been a giver. Maybe it was his turn to take? But that wasn't him.

A loud crack pulled him out of his thoughts. Once again he had forgotten reality by concentrating on something else. He jumped from the crate and stood in the middle of the ten by ten stall he had been exploring. He thought he had seen, along with the loud crack, the barn move. It did lean to one side quite a bit. It could fall in at any moment.

Jim laughed.

How ironic to have his life snuffed out by accident when shortly, no doubt, he'd bite the dust anyway. He wondered if it would be any easier to take if he were crushed rather than eaten away? Would Becky get over it faster? Would Brad? Mel? Ed?

The barn cracked again and Jim decided not to find out how everyone would react. He left. He unzipped his jacket and pulled off his gloves. The back of his pants felt damp. The sun had really warmed up the air. He scanned the hillside. Mel and Ed, at least, had the courtesy to let him be alone. Was it courtesy or respect? Either way was fine. In class, it might have turned into a discussion.

Jim entered the farmhouse just as he had the day before, through the downstairs window. It seemed brighter inside, although it probably wasn't. Maybe familiar was a better word.

This time he went into the kitchen and pulled the curtain inside. He took it down and put it in the sink. Now, from the hillside, there'd be nothing to display the house's emptiness. It could easily be occupied, as indeed Jim felt it must be, if not by the ghosts of the farmer and his wife, then by the ghosts of their memories.

Jim retraced his steps through the living room and up the stairs. For the second time in two days, he touched the quilt on the master bed, this time with tears in his eyes for the loss of love through death. But was love lost, he wondered, or merely lifted to a higher level of understanding? Would Brad have left behind the quilt that Jim and Becky used, if they both died? Did Brad see his parents' marriage as that loving? That important?

No. Jim felt sure of the answer. Brad had seen the ups and downs in his parents' relationship. He would have no unrealistic views of love from that perspective. But Jim still wished for romance in his death. There was love between him and Becky. He felt it. He hoped that Becky felt it as well. He lowered his head. He couldn't be sure of anything. Not these days.

Jim explored more of the bedroom than he had the day before, but found nothing more to reveal love—no pictures, no letters, or flattened flowers—and it saddened him. It made him feel that the quilt had been left by accident. Or that no one wanted it. Not because of what it stood for—love—but because of the death it symbolized.

He walked to the window and stood overlooking the field leading into the cool woods. A white glare rose off the snow. A light flurry of snow fell from a single dark cloud, which hung halfway over the field and the forest. Light from the sun poked through the cloud in clearly defined rays, reaching down like corridors between earth and sky. On the side of the hill, Jim saw a deer—a buck—and squinted to count the points. It seemed to be looking directly at him, then took off, brown-furred and white-tailed, to higher ground.

Jim ran past the bed, bumping his hip against the bedpost on his way. He leaped down the stairs without worrying about falling, and almost dived through the window. He didn't stop running until he reached the stone fence, where he bent down to spit and pant, his hands on his knees.

The deer was gone.

Could it be the same one? He didn't know.

He looked back at the house. It did look occupied now that the kitchen curtain wasn't hanging outside. He smiled and shook his head. Nowhere was the world more sensitive than in emptiness and in silence. His aloneness told him this. Tears welled up in him again. It was not the same deer, the same house, or the same day. How could he expect it to be? He wasn't the same.

At that moment, he felt more alone in the world than he had ever felt, even during his and Becky's brief separation. Even after Connie's death. His little girl.

He missed Connie's hand in his. Even around her friends she had been affectionate with him. Not like Brad, who always had appearances to keep up.

Jim shook his head. He knew that what he was about to

do would be fruitless, but he had to be sure. As the snow blew around him, he walked, a lone figure in a half-sunny snowstorm. From a distance, he would appear sad. The angle of his head and shoulders, his slow, defeated walk, would give him away. The fact that he carried no rifle during hunting season would confuse any onlooker.

Jim purposely selected the exact place where he had climbed over the stone fence the day before, to climb over it once again. Afterwards, he wound through the woods as closely repeating the previous day's path as possible. As the snow began to pick up, both in size of flake and density, Jim searched for the path he had taken and found nothing. Near the top of the hill, he resolved himself to failure and sat beneath a pine tree…and began to cry for the third time that morning. For once, he allowed the tears to come from self-pity. He didn't want the old barn to fall in. He didn't want the quilt to be left because using it would be too morbid. He didn't want the path to be gone, for the deer to be a memory. He didn't want to die.

The pain in his hip annoyed him. The cold ground made the bruise pulse. His whole body was a temple of physical, mental, and emotional pain. For once, he cried himself out. He was sick of being strong, of bucking up for other people.

When he was through, he stood up and walked. The snow fell all around him. In a clearing, the snowfall was difficult to see through, like a heavy fog on the highway. Jim turned his face to the sky and let the flakes fall onto his cheeks, his nose, his chin.

This might very well be my last winter on this earth. My last chance to feel the snow and breathe the winter air in the hills. He paused and enjoyed the moment.

Everything he'd known was about to be lost. Death brought with it the most profound changes—a child dies as a hero is born. Would he be a hero in the next life? Or another child? Miracles happen only once. There were no magic paths today. No talking deer.

When the cabin came into view, Jim slowed and sat on the side of the hill. He wanted the comfort that could be found inside, yet he didn't want it. He didn't want to lose what was outside—the winter. The season would be gone soon enough.

Chapter 3

The story was an odd one and no one believed it. Jim should have known that would include Becky. But why did he have to face it?

They sat together on the couch. "A dream," she said.

"No. It was real. I can't explain it, but it was."

"You couldn't find it the next day? The path, I mean."

"No." He quieted.

The television flashed. He pushed the mute button on the remote control. Uneven light patterns flitted across the screen, sweeps of light and shadow projected into the darkened living room.

"Then you dreamed it."

"Maybe I'm dreaming this, too."

"Don't do this."

"Do what? Ask my wife to believe what I tell her?"

"Remember what the psychiatrist said about your 'contact' with Connie?"

"How would he know?"

"It's his job to know."

"His job is to rationalize everything into his, and the majority's, idea of reality. There's no room for, for . . . "

"Miracles?" She smirked.

"For anything."

"So, now you've been a part of two miracles."

"No, not at all. Forget it, Becky."

"No. I want to hear it from you." She had always been the stronger fighter.

Jim was used to giving up before she did, but he didn't have to this time. It wasn't fair. "Connie was a phenomenon, a psychic one."

Becky didn't let him go on. "You called it a miracle then, just like you're calling this deer thing a miracle now."

"I was wrong," Jim said.

"You're adjusting your vocabulary to fit the purpose."

It wasn't true. "You don't have to believe me. Forget it." He fell quiet once again.

In a moment, Becky said, "Jimmy, I think you should go talk with Doctor Bauchman again."

Jim smiled. "I know you do. I should have expected it." He turned away.

She leaned closer, tried to get him to look at her again. "Don't be this way."

"There's no other way to be," he said.

"There is. You can be realistic. But you aren't; you're bull-headed."

"I know what I saw, what I heard. You don't have to believe me. I know."

"Then don't tell me." Becky got up and walked into the kitchen.

The wall switch clicked and a flood of light dumped into the living room. Jim shaded his eyes from the glare and turned his head away. A cabinet door plunked open and closed, then the refrigerator opened and closed. She poured something into a glass. There were no sounds for a while, until the glass was rinsed and set on the counter. The light went out and he heard Becky walk straight into the bedroom.

Jim hit the TV power button and stared into the light phosphorescent screen as it faded to black. The refrigerator kicked off. No noise came from the bedroom.

Becky would be in bed lying on her side, almost asleep.

He always envied her ability to drop off so quickly, while he took a half hour or more to fall asleep only to awaken easily throughout the night. He smiled, remembering how he got up to check the children when they were infants. As long as it was only a diaper change or a fresh bottle, he didn't burden Becky by awakening her. She used to get mad at him for letting her sleep, but he always enjoyed the time alone with Brad or Connie, sometimes both.

In an hour, he got up from the living room chair and fixed coffee. Sipping slowly, he stood in darkness by the window, looking into the street in front of the house. Their development was thirty-five years old. They bought the house when it was only a year old, from a salesman who had since transferred to Texas. They were in their mid-twenties then. Brad was almost two and Connie was due any day. They signed the mortgage agreement, and Connie was born two days later. With very little furniture and an income barely able to pay for the mortgage, utilities, and food, they moved in. The house had completed their happy family. Jim remembered him and Becky as being so much in love.

His job at the junior high school was relatively secure and he brought home a little extra money each month from working with the school newsletter and the annual magazine. He also helped with the student yearbook, collecting quotes from students by making it an assignment. He enjoyed it. His quiet disposition and willingness to observe the rules made him a hit with the school board, the superintendent, the principal, and his fellow teachers.

That night, though, it hardly mattered. Feeling death creeping up behind him, what mattered was that none of it would go on much longer. Initially, he had decided to have the lump removed, hoping he would be lucky and the doctors would get all the cancer at once. That was the first time. He knew now that without chemotherapy he would most likely die in less than twelve months. If a second lump returned it meant that the cancer had probably spread and that that would be the end of him. At that point, chemo seemed like a costly payment just to gain a few months of life. But now, those months seemed important. He wasn't afraid to die; he just wanted a little more time. So much in his life was uncompleted. He had people he wanted to talk with before he died. He wanted time to spend with his son, his friends, even Becky. He owed so much more than time to Becky. He wanted to let her know more about him, how he felt. Even if it was no longer possible, he wanted to balance things out.

A car went around the corner, up the street, and for a moment he stood bathed in light. Shadows scurried across the wall behind him, in and out of the house. The momentary exposure to light unsettled him. He let the feeling of darkness hold him. There was such comfort in darkness, an inexplicable sensation of closeness.

His thoughts returned to the deer.

What was he, a fifty-eight-year-old schoolteacher meant to do with such a sign? He could better understand Connie spending time with him after her death. That was personal contact with the other side. He had never tried to gain any deeper meaning from it. It seemed simple then. She was helping him get over her death, letting him know that she was all right. Lately, he thought she might be preparing him for his own death.

Jim closed the front curtain and finished his coffee. Taking a light jacket from the hall closet, he stepped outside onto the stoop. A chill wind swept over him and he contemplated returning to the warm living room. But the cold wouldn't hurt him; nothing could, except the disbelief of his friends and family. He'd already gone through that about Connie, and he'd just learned to avoid certain subjects. Maybe he'd do the same with the deer. Forget talking about it, just live with it, inside. Everything didn't have to be in the open all the time. He'd had his secrets in the past.

Jim stepped off the stoop and took a short walk up the street. Some houses were lighted inside like Christmas trees; others stood dark as tunnels. Each home had its own occupants who struggled with their own problems. Some of those people might even have it worse than he and Becky. Brad was worried about losing his job when things got rough. Life without work probably looked worse to Brad than death looked to Jim. Brad might lose his car, his home, and possibly his wife. How unnecessary all that would be.

Jim's shoulders rippled with goose bumps. He tried to tighten the jacket's flimsy collar, but it kept flopping down in the wind.

The cold represented the earth, the climate, reality. It was life affirming. That's what Jim looked for in everything: affirmation. The lights, the cars, the cold. If the deer were real, were they another step, another representation of after-life affirmation? If they were real? Why would he doubt himself? *They were real*, he thought. They were the gift. And what a gift. An entire afternoon of nothing short of miracle. All the deer at the end, coming out of the mist.

A wind gust hit Jim hard as he turned the corner at the end of his street. A big chunk of snow, from a nearby rooftop, made a crunching sound when it hit the ground. The cold struck his face and neck and quickly moved down inside his jacket. The clouds overhead rushed across the sky, mimicking time. Was a leisurely walk a wise thing to do? Had hunting been wise? The lost time. The lost time. Should he have spent some of it with Brad or Becky? Had he wasted time he could have spent with Connie before she died?

He had more questions about his life than he had life left to answer them. Questions of the universe and questions of a personal nature. And they could all be expanded or contracted to suit his mood. But the deer, what was their personal message? Life, all life, exists as one? That's universal. What about the personal? He thought about what Ed had told him, that he had always been a giver, but what did that mean? A giver. So what? An affirmation of a personal trait. Fine. Maybe it was that simple.

He turned the corner again, and, off the main street, the houses cut the wind's strength. Clouds still rushed overhead. In the window of one house, Jim noticed a family watching television and wondered if that wasn't better than reading, which is what he had always promoted in his own family. At least this family shared something.

On his final stretch toward his house, Jim held the collar of the jacket near his neck. Soon his neck and the backs of his hands in contact with it became warm. He could make another trip around, watch the clouds roll out some more. Becky would be asleep anyhow. But it was too cold. He could switch to a heavier coat, but he knew that, once inside, he would want to sit down, maybe go to bed himself.

When he did get back inside the house, he felt tired. He could go to bed, but he didn't want the night drifting away without him. He looked in on Becky and then sat in the recliner in the living room. Staring at the ceiling, he fell asleep.

The sound of screeching tires awoke him. It was still dark. His mind was on Connie and, for a moment, he wasn't sure whether he actually heard the tires or dreamed them. When he heard them a second time, he sat up. His neck hurt from sleeping with his head tilted to one side. He rubbed his neck and stood up. His back hurt too. When he turned around, Becky stood in the dimness of the hall nightlight.

"You shouldn't sleep out here so often," she said.

Her robe was parted at the neck and her hair was pulled back. Jim always admired the fine bone structure in her face. Without makeup, in the dim light, it was even more apparent. "Did I wake you, dear?"

"No, it was those kids screeching their tires. Someone should call the cops."

"It's over before it's begun. They'd never catch them," he said.

"I know. Just once would be nice, though."

"I agree." He rubbed his back a little and pushed his chest out to stretch the muscles.

"Will you come to bed now?"

"Sure. What time is it?"

"Almost three-thirty. You've only got a few hours."

"I hope I'm not too tired tomorrow," he said.

"Did you sleep okay out here?"

"Until the noise."

"You should be fine."

He followed her back to bed.

In the morning, Jim rose, showered, shaved, and was sitting in the kitchen having coffee by the time Becky got up. She sat down with him, coffee cup in hand. "I'm sorry about the deer," she said.

"About them?"

"Miracles are difficult to believe unless they're yours. The deer talking, that happened to you. I don't have that closeness you do with nature. I wish I did." She stroked his hand.

He turned his palm up so they could hold hands.

"It's your miracle. I'm sorry if I was insensitive about it. But it's yours. I don't know what to do with it. It's for you to figure out. My frustration got the best of me."

Jim smiled and shook her hand, grasping it firmly. "I'm alone on this one."

"I'll listen, but don't expect me to be able to believe as easily as you do."

"I won't." He turned his head away. She was trying hard. He wasn't sure he deserved it.

"I know you feel alone in all of this. I'm not faced with it like you are. But I can be here. I can listen. I can hold you, if that's what you need." Her voice cracked.

"You can?" He still looked away. They hadn't been that close for years, he thought.

"Yes."

He almost broke down. If he was the giver, shouldn't he be doing something for her?

"You have to open up to me again," she said.

There were tears in her eyes, small ones, revealing a quiet sadness. They didn't have a lot of time. Was she feeling it too? Jim patted her cheek. "I'll try. I will. It's just that. . ."

"That was years ago. After Connie, I ignored you, pushed you away. Even through that, through everything, you gave as much as you could." Now Becky turned away. "You stayed, and you didn't have to."

"There's history here," he told her.

"But there was a future there, with her. I've given you neither. I'm sorry."

"We've been fine," he said.

"We've been courteous. You deserve it to be more loving, before . . ."

"Before I die." He finished her sentence.

Regardless what he said, Jim wasn't so sure that either one of them could become loving again. The reasons why he felt that way didn't matter any longer. Sometimes he wanted it to go on just as it was.

"I'm just fine," he said.

"Then I need it to be more loving," she said.

"But it can't come from pity. I don't know if we can do it." She had just admitted that she couldn't believe him, trust his words, his experiences. Could she, then, trust his love, even if he could open up again?

Before he left for school that morning he promised her he'd try. Although he wasn't sure how to attempt to try. "Open up" sounded so simple, like open up a can of soup, or the cabinet, the car door. But she wanted more, his heart maybe, or his soul. But his soul contained Connie and the deer.

Deer, he thought. Even the word was both singular and plural. One could not open up without the other. Half a flower opening to the sun would not be as beautiful. He and Becky had to open together, then. Would that ever happen? It all had to happen together, making each of them the gift and the giver?

Chapter 4

During his first two classes Jim operated out of an unusual trance-like state. Half his mind was on his teaching, while half his mind was meditating on his recent experiences. One student in his second class asked if he was all right. The boy had been on his way out to his next class, but by the time Jim registered the question, the classroom was empty.

Third hour was Jim's planning period, so he locked his room and went down to the teachers' lounge to relax. The halls of the school were littered with artwork, essays on the environment, fall leaves and colors, announcements for band, wrestling, basketball, the chess club, the science club. Several students said hello to Jim as he made his way to the lounge. Once there, he poured himself coffee and sat on the sofa to think. Two women teachers, Beth and

Phyllis, were the only others in the lounge with him. Jim listened halfheartedly to their conversation, something about the pep-rally eating into certain class periods—always the same ones — and putting those students' grades and final test scores in jeopardy.

It all seemed so insignificant. He had a similar problem with peprallies interfering with his classes, of course, but he piled on the homework and pushed his students a little harder in the classes they did have to keep up with the curriculum. In the span of a lifetime what were five or ten class periods equal to? A weekend? Then again, he'd give a lot for an extra weekend.

Phyllis sat down next to him and put her hand on his knee. "How are you feeling?"

Jim was slightly surprised to have Phyllis sit with him. Beth poured herself a second cup of coffee. "I'm fine," Jim said.

After the short-lived scandal, many of the women teachers refused to even make eye contact. For a short time the men winked at him as they passed him in the halls. He wasn't exactly proud of himself.

Now Phyllis was actually sitting next to him. Friendly? More than likely it was either pity or curiosity. He had known news of the cancer would leak out. His first trip to the hospital had raised eyebrows, and the busybodies in the front office were, well, busybodies. He couldn't keep his insurance forms a secret. He thought of the secretaries in the front office. With secret being the root word, they sure weren't able to keep any. Jim laughed to himself.

"Something funny?" Phyllis asked.

Jim turned to her. "No. Not that I can think of."

"We're sorry to hear you may have to go back into the

hospital."

"Thank you." He imagined, from what little he knew of Phyllis, that she might even be glad that he had a disease. She could say to herself with no little satisfaction, that adulterers get their due reward eventually.

He had briefly entertained similar thoughts himself. But of all the wrongs done in the world, a short affair with an assistant teacher didn't seem punishable by death. He just happened to be one of the many people who got cancer. That was it. Not punishment. More like a disease lottery.

Phyllis fidgeted for a moment. Jim's answers were much too direct. "So, everything's all right at home then? With Becky, I mean?"

"Perfect," he said. "One thing did happen recently, though."

Phyllis perked up. She turned toward him.

Jim didn't know what made him do it. He was just sick of all the cattiness. His life was his own. He and Becky had their own problems to overcome. Let Phyllis think about this: "During my hunting trip last week, I talked with deer."

"Oh." She seemed uninterested, as though he were spoofing her. She began to stand and he placed his hand on her forearm to stop her. "One moment. You don't seem to understand. I met up with three deer in the woods, one buck and two doe. They talked with me."

"It figures," he heard Beth say from across the room.

"They talked with me all afternoon and they left me with a sign. They said I was the gift and the giver. What do you think of that? What do you suppose that means? Really? I've been trying to figure it out for days now."

Phyllis forced her way out of her seat against his hand. "I wouldn't know."

"Ask around. I'm looking for suggestions."

Phyllis and Beth scooted out the door.

Jim sat back in the sofa and sipped at the last of his coffee. He felt better for some reason. He'd held so much in these past years. Who cared if he finally let loose? Who cared what they thought? They'd make their own decisions about him when he was gone anyway. *Let them start now*, he thought. He was crazy. Let them think it.

Chapter 5

That Thursday Jim went into the hospital to have the second lump removed. Becky showed up in the hospital room after work, still dressed in a navy-colored silk jacket and slacks, a ruffled shirt of light blue and green, and navy shoes. Jim felt groggy, and a bit sore from the operation.

"How you doing?" Becky said.

Jim opened his eyes and shifted into a more comfortable position. "Tired."

She touched his arm. "Brad'll be here pretty soon with Susan."

"They don't have to bother."

"They want to."

He turned his head. His breathing became heavy, one sigh after another.

"So," Becky said in preparation.

Jim waited to hear it, whatever it was that bothered her. After so many years of living together, he knew what to expect just by her movements, sighs, and sound of her voice. At these familiar moments she looked older to him. The face he loved took on harsh angles. Even her mouth moved differently across words she'd used on countless other occasions.

"I heard about you telling everybody at school about this deer thing."

"Doesn't take long, does it?"

"Why did you do it?"

"I told Phyllis. She was nosing around and I just got fed up. She and Beth were the only two there." His words trailed off toward the end.

Becky shook her head at him, but he hardly noticed. There was no reason for him to care. That's how he saw it. Becky was being overly sensitive to his actions because of what happened before. Once he died, though, she'd be pretty much cut off from the school altogether. That'd be it. To hell with them. He didn't say any of that though. Besides, he felt much too tired to go over it all with her.

"They probably think I'm crazy for being with you. Or maybe they pity me. I don't need either, you know?" Her voice was directed at him, but her words got garbled on their way over.

Jim knew what was up, even if he heard only part of what she said. He was just too tired to think, and too disgusted at this point with his own life, to care what anyone said, thought, felt, or dreamed up. It was his life. His miracle. There were cases, documented ones, where people lifted cars to save loved ones, or fell from planes and lived, or even died and came back to life. All miracles. Accepted ones. So what was wrong with his?

He had decided to celebrate his miracle rather than hide in it. A wonderful thing happened. He was through with keeping low key so other people felt better about themselves.

"What have you got to say? Can't you tell Phyllis you were joking?"

Jim's eyes opened and he looked straight at Becky. "It really happened."

"Oh. So that's it?"

"Thass it."

"Maybe when you're off your pain medicine and back to normal you'll think differently."

"I won't."

"You'd better."

He turned his head. On the one hand, he wanted the two of them to be close again. He'd do almost anything to make her happy. On the other hand, he had a right to his opinions and his experiences. No one could take them away. And he'd tell her, except that words took too much energy. He didn't have the strength. He did get the energy to tell Becky that he'd changed his mind about chemotherapy. He was willing to go through a few treatments, "Just to see," he said.

Her expression changed. "Jimmy, are you sure?" Her face lit up. "I'm glad." She wanted him to try. Maybe there was a reason now. Before, she felt he wanted to die so that he could be with Connie. But now. . .

She remembered their talk earlier in the week. Maybe he

wanted to be with her. She hoped so. Through everything they'd overcome, it seemed a waste not to try. She still wanted to be there for him. She still loved him. "But I'd still like you to deal with Phyllis. I hate what they might think." She came over and fluffed his pillow for him. "Tell me you'll talk with her."

Jim began to speak, but Brad and Susan came into the room, bringing the cold and excitement of the outside world with them.

Brad pulled off his gloves and took Susan's coat, then he removed his own. In the midst of the commotion, he hugged his mother and kissed her on the cheek. Susan did the same. There was hardly enough room for the three of them, the bed took up so much space. There was so much confusion that Jim just closed his eyes until they all became situated.

"So, how you feeling, Pop?" Brad pushed at his father's leg.

Jim opened his eyes. "Hi, Son. Hi, Susan."

"Hi, Jim. How's it going?" Susan never called him Dad after she and Brad were married, and Jim was thankful for that small, but significant, courtesy. Especially now, after Connie's death.

He really liked Susan. She was perfect for Brad, even though Brad wasn't always sure of the fact. "I'm doing fine," Jim told her. "Feeling better all the time."

"He's agreed to try chemotherapy," Becky announced to confirm what Jim told Susan.

"Great news, Dad." Brad grabbed Susan's hand in excitement. He looked at his father seriously. "We want you around for a long time."

"We need to talk more, Brad. There're things I'd like to talk about with you."

"I agree. Let's start as soon as you're out of here," Brad said.

Jim nodded slowly. His energy waned.

"Don't talk now," Becky told him. "You'll have time later."

Chapter 6

Once Jim got out of the hospital, Brad had trouble adjusting his schedule so that they could get together. Not visit, that still went on, but actually sit down one-on-one and talk. It wasn't until after Jim's first chemotherapy experience that Becky created enough fuss over Brad's lack of commitment that Brad thought to get further involved. The chemo brought back all the reality of the situation, the seriousness of the disease.

So, one Saturday Brad and Jim headed for the hunting cabin. For two days. The weekend would be enough time. Jim was tired, but thought he'd make it fine. Becky was concerned but trusted her son to keep her husband safe.

Brad let Jim drive the first hour then took over for the last half of the trip. "The mountains sure are beautiful, aren't they, Dad?"

"Yes, even without leaves on the trees. There's something beautiful in their absence, in knowing that spring will bring them back. The return of life," he added.

Brad looked sideways at Jim, curious to see his expression. But there was no expression on Jim's face to lead to any conclusion, so Brad turned his attention back to the road. "You said, have been saying, that we should talk, but you never lead me into conversation, anything we haven't said before, or couldn't discuss with Mom and Sue around."

Jim looked out the window, the scenery breezing past in a never-ending stream. "It takes time, Son. We have to ease into it. It's like love making: if it's jumped into too quickly, it's instinct, sex—but properly paced, it's a joining of souls, it's love." Jim couldn't believe he'd said what he'd said. He had been thinking about Becky and him, and felt a little embarrassed.

"Where'd that come from?"

"I don't know. But it's true. Those are the things people don't talk about, don't get serious enough about. And it's important."

"It is," Brad agreed.

Jim looked at his son. He was a man, another grown man with a wife and a home and problems of his own. Jim could remember the boy, but didn't feel he knew the man well enough. Jim knew his own friends, Mel and Ed, better than he knew his son. "Tell me," he said finally, "do you talk to Susan about the difference?"

"The difference?"

"Between love and sex?"

"We talk about it. I guess."

"And?"

"Dad, is this what you wanted to get into?"

"Not exactly, but yes, this too."

"Why's it so important?" Brad asked.

Jim sat forward in his seat and leaned around so he could see Brad's face. "I want to know my own son before I die."

"Did you know Connie this well?"

That was a difficult question for Jim. It hurt. He and Connie had a special, private relationship. One he'd never shared. Yet Brad was only trying to know his father, Jim thought. Equal sharing. That's what the trip was meant to be. "Yes, I think I did."

"All those long talks in the den?" Brad said.

"Yes, and walks at night. Remember?"

"I think Mom used to get jealous. Mom knew Connie told you things she wouldn't tell her."

"Becky was always so judgmental. She'd decide what was right, then tell you kids what to do, instead of help you figure out what was best for you."

"Even me and Con would talk about it. Mom would say, 'No, you did the wrong thing,' and you'd say, 'So, is that what you had hoped as an outcome and how did you feel about yourself afterwards?' We used to laugh about it." Brad shook his head. "I miss her, Dad."

"So do I. A lot."

"Is that why you and that woman at school did what you did?"

Another rough question. Jim wondered how long Brad had held that question inside. "I didn't do that because of Connie. Not at all." He shook his head and Brad waited to hear more, giving Jim plenty of space to talk. "There was a gap then, between me and your mother. Out of grief or cowardice or something. Neither of us attempted to fill it. I turned to someone else. It could have happened to either one of us at the time."

"But it didn't."

Was that judgmental or was it just a statement? Did Brad get that trait from Becky? "You don't know that to be true, Brad."

"Did she?"

"I'm just saying that you don't know." Jim was firm.

"Aren't people supposed to hold tighter during rough times?"

All of a sudden, Jim knew that Brad was concerned for himself. Would the same thing happen to Susan and him? "They're supposed to. But, until they're tested, you never know how two people might react."

"You guys had been through rough times before. You'd think you'd have learned to come together automatically," Brad said.

"That would have been nice. I'm not proud of what happened. It's created its own problems since then."

"I can imagine. But, you know, Mom was always a little jealous of Con. Maybe your overwhelming sorrow frightened her and made her back away."

Overwhelming sorrow, Jim thought. Is that how Brad saw his father during that time? "Let's not blame her. It takes two. I didn't look to her for comfort either. That was the worst time in my life."

"I'm sorry." Brad watched the road. "Now isn't?"

Jim felt pride that his son could be so open with him. "Not now. In a way I'm getting to explore life."

"You've thought about death a lot too since this started?" Brad asked.

"I have."

"Does it disrupt your day an awful lot? How do you ever concentrate on anything else?"

"Oh, I do. I do." Jim sat back in his seat once again to relax, accepting the new line of conversation. "I see everything clearer now. I tend to experience the now more than I've ever done. That may sound odd, but if you think about it, aren't you always in the past or future, some other place?"

"How do you mean?"

"Simple. When you're at work, you're thinking ahead. When will this project end? When will the day be over? Or you're in the past. About that fight you had with Susan that morning. Or the love making. How often do you actually notice your desk? The walls? Do you have a radio in your office?" Jim asked.

"Yes."

"Can you honestly say that you hear it all day?"

"No, of course not," Brad said.

"And a window?" Jim asked.

"You're right, Dad. Sometimes it'll begin to snow and I won't notice until one of the secretaries steps in and tells me."

"Exactly. Did you know that most people begin to get depressed Sunday afternoon about three o'clock, just in anticipation of Monday morning?"

"Really?"

"It's true. And their weekend isn't even over. They've got a good seven or eight hours left to enjoy it."

"A full work day," Brad said.

"That's right."

"But you can't be present, in the present, one hundred percent of the time. Isn't it our ability to compare past and present, and to project into the future what makes us human? Isn't it all part of being intelligent?" Brad asked.

"But it was never meant to reduce the present to nothing. Or, if we're being fair, to only a few moments a day," Jim argued.

"Stop and smell the roses."

"Maybe."

"So," Brad turned to his father, "how do we live more in the present?"

"I don't know if I can tell you. You may have to learn on your own. But one thing's for sure, I've been doing more of it. I think getting into the woods helps. The only thing around is the present. Hunters may have something there, something they didn't know they had, a link to the present. No wonder it's so attractive to some people."

"So, are you noticing the drive?"

"Of course. Maybe more than you. But also, I'm here with you. Listening to the way you speak, watching how you turn your head. I listen closely to your words. I know what your face looks like when you're embarrassed and when you're interested. I can tell when you're not listening, too."

"Uh, oh."

"You laugh just like when you were a little boy," Jim said. "You haven't changed in that way. Sometimes I'd hear you downstairs watching cartoons or something on a Saturday morning, and you'd laugh. Becky and I would look at each other and just break up."

Brad kept his eyes on the road and made the turn to go up to the cabin.

"Didn't mean to embarrass you," Jim said.

"You didn't really. Well, maybe a little. I just never realized, never knew how you felt. You never said."

"There's always been a lot I loved about you. I'm proud of how you grew up. You're a good man. I think the easiest way to tell is by watching Susan."

"Why?"

"The way she listens to you when you speak. How she takes your hand when you reach for her. She's comfortable in being part of your life. Regardless of your minor differences, and I'm sure you have them, you have a mutual respect there, a closeness."

Brad brought the car to a stop next to the cabin. "I would never have guessed you'd be able to notice so much from a few seemingly small acts." He nodded. "Thank you for noticing."

Jim smiled. Brad had a few wrinkles around his eyes and laugh lines, too, around his mouth. He had the kind of face that made people feel at home. Even though Jim recognized parts of himself in Brad's face—his nose and chin—Becky's influence lighted Brad's eyes and mouth, which created that friendly look Brad carried with him. Those same features had made Connie stunning, and probably helped cause some of her problems while growing up. Brad handled his appearance well. Jim was sure Susan appreciated that fact as much as he and Becky did.

Brad got out of the car and opened the trunk. The day was mild. Snow covered the ground even though no new snow had fallen for a few weeks. Sunrise had already overcome the trees to the east, and placed golden strips of light, like spotlights leading the way up to the cabin door. Brad removed things from the trunk and walked up to the cabin. Turning to make sure his father was behind him, Brad squinted his eyes. "You have the keys, don't you?"

"I thought *you* had them!"

"Really, Dad."

"Always on my key ring," Jim said. He opened the door and they both stepped into the dampness of the uninhabited room.

"It's really cold in here."

Jim laughed. "Make a fire."

"Are we staying in?"

"We'll be gone a few hours at best," Jim said. "The place will be warm when we get back."

Jim unpacked the groceries and put their extra clothes in the small closet in the bedroom. He threw sheets on the beds, too. By the time he finished, Brad had a strong fire going in the fireplace. "We could have used those heaters," he said, pointing to two space heaters in the corner of the room.

"I like the fire better," Jim told him. "Let's say we grab something light and take a walk. I want to show you something."

"What's that?"

"I'll show you."

After a quick breakfast, the two of them dressed appropriately for the mild temperatures outside and left the cabin.

"You think the fire'll be okay?" Brad said, running to catch up with Jim.

"Yes, I'm sure." Jim had already crossed the small clearing and entered the woods.

"The snow's hard to walk in with this top crust. You break though a second after your weight is on your foot. It's weird."

"Surprises you, doesn't it?" Jim said.

"Yeah."

"I'm going to take you around the hill to the valley. It opens up into some old fields. There's a deserted farm there." Jim's pace remained steady and his eyes focused on his objective.

Brad had a rough time with the terrain. Years of sidewalks and shopping malls made him not want to raise his feet enough. He tripped every few steps until he learned to lift his feet higher than he was accustomed to.

Jim smiled to himself as he walked ahead, leading the way.

"Is this place abandoned?" Brad asked.

"More or less."

"There're people living there?"

"Ghosts maybe."

"Dad."

While growing up, Brad had been primarily influenced by Becky. Possibly they had developed the same connection Jim and his daughter experienced. Jim knew Brad didn't believe in him talking to Connie any more than Becky did.

"Okay, it's abandoned," Jim said, "for all practical purposes."

The fields and the farm came into view as Jim and Brad made the turn along the hill. The sun did a fine job lighting the area. *Anyone would have to fall in love with a place like this,* Jim thought. Jim stopped to let Brad catch up.

Brad stood beside his father on the hillside. "It's beautiful."

"Now do you know why I hunt here?"

"Hike, Dad. Now I know why you come here. I would too." He put his hand on Jim's shoulder. "I will from now on."

Jim patted Brad's hand. "Let's go."

Brad kept up with Jim on the trip down toward the house and barn. They helped one another over the stone fence while the sun warmed them.

"So," Jim said while crossing through the field with his son, "do you and Susan talk about sex and love? The differences?"

"You must be murder on the kids in school."

"Hey, I just don't forget unanswered questions that easily."

Brad had been loosening up since the trip began and was able to joke with his father almost like he would his own friends. Only a slight weight of parental respect kept Brad from pushing the conversation into cruder territory, but it was better not to go there anyway. It was less honest, less serious, than where his father headed the conversation. "To answer the question directly: yes, we do."

"You do or you have?"

"Semantics."

"Not really." Jim stopped to look at his son. "It's an important question. I'm learning that you have to continue talking. I believe that's something Becky and I have failed to do. You wouldn't say something simple like, 'I love you,' just once and expect it to be over." He looked into Brad's face. His son listened closely, watched his father's lips move as he spoke.

"You're right, Dad. And we do talk about it." Brad swallowed. "Regularly. Ever since we learned about your . . . incident."

"My affair."

"It made me wonder about our relationship, so Susan and I talk about it. At first she got annoyed with me. It's difficult to talk about. It brings out a lot of feelings, makes you vulnerable. You're right. Saying 'I love you' is simple. It's too simple. Each person decides what it means and forgets that the other person might not think the same way. When you talk about love, really talk about it, you start to explore more deeply. And love and sex aren't always that close. But if there's love, real love, then there's no sex without including that love. If the love's not real, I'm convinced that there is only sex. The important element is missing."

"It's the difference between cutting down a field of wheat to clear land for a ball field and clearing it to feed yourself and your family for the winter," Jim said.

"Maybe." Brad began to walk toward the house again.

"You don't like my analogy?"

"I don't know. I see your point though. One act has so much more behind it, a purpose, so to speak, at least in reference to the wheat. The kids who would use the baseball field have a purpose too. You know what, though?" Brad said.

"What's that?"

"I would never want to have sex without love. I don't mean the words or the feelings. I mean the understanding. Susan can say, 'I love you' all she wants, and she can actually love me so much, and in just the right ways for me, and it still wouldn't be enough."

"Then what is enough?" Jim asked.

"You have to talk about it, explain it from every angle. Actually sit on the floor together, or the bed, the couch, but together, not across the kitchen table for God's sake." He was excited about the conversation now. "You have to talk so that you begin to understand. That's what does it. It's the weight of understanding that makes the difference. When Susan comes to me I know that she brings the words of poems and the colors of her favorite painting with her. She brings the cat she loved when she was a little girl and the children we'll have one day. With all that present, there couldn't be more love. There's better sex because of the love, because of the understanding."

"Wow."

"Sorry, Dad, for going on so much."

"That's all right. I processed what you said as quickly as I could. You seem to have thought about this, explored it more than I have."

"You think? You and Mom have been together a long time. You've made it."

"And I think we grew out of what you're talking about before we could grow into it. We've talked — don't get me wrong. You learn a lot about a person in all those years. But I may have missed in my own life the point I was trying to make with you. It seems I'm learning more from our time together than I thought. I thought I'd be able to teach a little too. Now I'm not so sure."

"You listen. So many people don't. I learned that from you. It's always been your greatest gift."

Jim lowered his head. For him, the trip had already been a success. Anything more would be a bonus, extra credit.

Once they got to the porch, their conversation switched to the old house. Brad was really taken by it, its look and its feel. Much more taken than Jim had expected him to be. In fact, Brad approached the place with an interest and enthusiasm mirroring Jim's when he first discovered it.

"Wow, check it out inside, Dad. There's still some furniture in there." Brad looked in the window, one hand on either side of the sill, holding his body back from falling inside. "Have you been inside?"

"Yes, through that window, actually."

"Doesn't the door work?" Brad asked.

"You know, I never tried it."

"Let's." Brad went to the door and pulled on the handle. It was locked or nailed shut, but wiggled on its hinges. Brad ran his hand around it, looking for the place it was secured. It wouldn't matter. It would still be closed to them, but Brad's curiosity made him explore it. "It's nailed shut at the top. That's why it wiggles so much, but won't open." He seemed completely satisfied just to know. "Your instincts were right, Dad. We'll take the window."

Brad climbed through as Jim watched. They had a similar build. Jim always thought of it as average. Not intimidating, nor wimpy. Brad's youth, though, was clearly expressed in his speed and agility, even through he wasted movements in turning this way or that—all expressions of excitement escaping through the energy of the body. Jim watched Brad explore the house in almost the exact sequence he'd followed the first time.

"From the hill," Brad said while creeping up the stairs, "this place looks inhabited."

Jim remembered the curtain he had pulled down in the kitchen and was glad he did.

"I can see why you'd say the house isn't quite deserted. It looks occupied, there's furniture, and," he stopped suddenly, "even the bed's made. That's really odd. Who'd do that?"

"Maybe it was just left that way," Jim suggested. "After all, the furniture and everything. . . "

Brad touched the quilt and walked up the side of the bed sliding his hand along it. "It's kind of romantic, isn't it, Dad? Is that what you thought?"

"I did. Either that, or morbid."

"No, romantic. I bet the old couple died together in this bed."

Jim watched his son's facial expressions as they changed

from interest, to excitement, to seriousness. Brad thought deeply about things Jim hadn't imagined he would. About such things he himself thought deeply, things he paid attention to.

"Dad, did you look out this window?" Brad motioned for Jim to come closer.

Jim could feel he son's energy as they stood together, side by side, looking out the second story window of the old farmhouse.

"It's beautiful," Brad said. "What a view they had of their land when they were lying in bed."

Making love, Jim thought, and knew that Brad was thinking the same thing.

Chapter 7

They didn't explore the barn that Saturday, but they did go through the house more thoroughly than Jim had done by himself. He followed Brad into the attic and the basement, through each bedroom. They talked for hours about Brad's job, and Jim's, about their life together while Brad was growing up. About Connie.

Brad had loved his sister, and the closeness between Brad and his father took on a new closeness. Jim felt comfortable sharing Connie's and his secrets with Brad. In fact, he felt such relief telling Brad about her that it brought her back into reality for a brief time. Jim explained about her difficulties making and keeping friends. How the other girls' boyfriends would say how pretty she was and how her friends would then blame her. He even told Brad how she came to him the first time she made love to a boy. Jim almost cried, remembering her hurt and confusion.

Jim and Brad kept talking during the walk back to the cabin and throughout their late lunch. Brad told Jim that he was amazed at how well Jim handled Connie's small disasters—that's what Brad called them, small disasters—and that he was proud of Jim for not scolding her for decisions already made. Jim glowed in his son's praise.

After lunch, Jim cleaned and arranged one of the beds for a short nap. He felt more tired than he thought he would from the morning's excursion. Brad cleaned up the dishes from lunch and dusted the cabin quickly before settling down to read a book. When Jim appeared again, Brad was asleep on the raggedy couch that protruded from the wall near the fireplace, which still blazed warmly, pushing yellow-orange light into the room. Jim quietly put on some warm clothes, then went outside, shutting the door behind him. The weather had turned cold, but felt good on his face. He decided to take a short walk into the woods. Five or ten minutes. Jim knew that if Brad woke up, he'd be worried, so the walk would have to be close by.

The sun angled down from the far west over the tree line, which cast shadows, long and deep, into the woods. Shivers ran up his spine and his hands shook as he entered the woods. He shrugged off his reactions. He glanced at his watch and calculated that it'd get completely dark in an hour, an hour and a half, maybe earlier in the woods. But he'd be ten minutes at most.

These woods had always been familiar to him. Why he had waited so long to explore the old house, he didn't know. One reason, of course, was that it had been occupied until only a few years previous. Now, he wished he'd taken the time to visit the people who'd lived there. But why?

He let his thoughts wander, reviewing his day with Brad. Contrary to how he told Brad he paid much more attention to the now, Jim skirmished in that recent past like a child playing along the beach. When he looked at his watch once again, almost forty minutes had gone by. He had to turn back.

As he rested for a moment against a bare maple tree, he heard walking. Expecting it to be Brad, he waited. A few more steps and Jim saw it. A doe. It looked directly at him. Familiar? When he moved, it stepped away, but it didn't run. He moved again, this time toward it a few steps. It stepped away also, matching him for distance. He spoke, "Are you the deer who . . .?" The deer's ears lifted in curiosity, its head turned away. "Don't!" Jim followed it into the woods, watching closely as its white tail bobbed deeper into the darkness. He ran as fast as he could, but the doe disappeared ahead of him.

His head lowered, he walked back to where he had been, then got the idea to look for a path. Magically, as he scanned the area, the path appeared one place, then appeared somewhere else. First it led between two pines, then near a pile of old leaves, around a gully, then past some bushes. Everywhere Jim looked he saw the possibility of a path. But the deer had gone on behind him. He turned around and again found the possibility of one path after another. This time he decided to go deeper into the woods, follow where he last remembered seeing the doe. Maybe the path would become more visible.

At several places Jim was sure he had come across the right path, but each time it fizzled out into thickets or groves of trees, which left no indication of a place well traveled by anything. Overhead, the sky, patched with areas of clouds and blue like a quilt, still held onto the last luminescent flicker of the setting sun. Jim shook his head and began to cry. He wanted the deer back! If he were, in fact, *the giver*, why couldn't he give himself this one small thing? *One last time,* he thought. *One last time.* He shivered and pulled his jacket close to his neck. This had become a familiar activity of his, trying to keep warm in the cold world. He shook his head at his own tendency toward melodrama, then turned towards the cabin.

For a short while he was lost, disoriented really, for he knew the woods well. Once he got his bearings any nervousness due to his confusion in the darkness subsided and he plodded on back to the cabin. He tired more quickly now than when he searched the deer's whereabouts, and rested regularly. When he rounded a small grove of trees, he heard Brad yelling.

"Dad!"

Jim looked at his watch, but it was too dark to read the dial. He yelled back, "Brad."

"Dad?"

"Where are you?" Jim yelled.

"I'll keep talking."

Jim followed Brad's half-yells until he saw, in a short distance, a flashlight beam. It is easy to misinterpret the direction of voices while in the woods, but not their volume. Jim edged closer by concentrating on the loudness of Brad's voice. "Brad, over here."

Brad turned around several times until, moving more slowly, Jim could say, "This way." Brad followed his flashlight beam, and soon the two men were side by side.

"I was worried sick. Where the hell were you?" Brad said.

"Walking. I guess I misjudged the time it would take to get dark. I'm surprised you didn't get lost. I know these woods," Jim said.

"What if you collapsed or something?"

"I get tired sometimes. I don't collapse." Jim held back telling Brad just how tired he got, or how easy it would have been to just settle in comfortably next to a tree and sleep, which was what he wanted most at the time.

"We'd better get back," Brad said. He looked around. "Which way?"

They both laughed. "This way," Jim said, taking the lead. "It's a good thing you found me."

It was only a ten-minute walk back to the cabin, the same distance Jim had expected to go as he began his short walk. That was before he saw the deer. And now, halfway back, he wanted to return to the woods. The feeling grew inside him like a tidal wave. The silence, broken only by their footfalls, made the feeling grow and grow, and as the impulse to turn and run back into the woods increased, Jim's pace slowed.

Brad finally broke the silence, shattering Jim's growing need to go back like a fallen glass on a stone patio. "You getting tired, Dad?"

"No. No, I'm not." Jim picked up the pace.

"Were you looking for them?" Brad blurted out, his voice violating the dark woods. He held the flashlight to the side, shining it beyond Jim, but in front of him. Jim had never reached for it, not requiring its security.

What had Becky told him? Had the two of them discussed his

encounter with the deer, as he and Connie would have done had it been Becky who had the experience? But Brad had asked the question. Was it innocent or an accusation? Was it judgmental? Jim wanted to know what Brad's tone of voice indicated, but just as quickly didn't care. The experience had been a miracle. If he wanted to chase it, who could say he was wrong in doing so? "Yes," he admitted.

"Why?"

The question proved a lack of understanding — Becky's influence once again. Did he think his father crazy? Did Becky think that? Jim wasn't sure how to respond if judgment had already been cast. The cabin came into view. The lights were on inside and the fire pushed smoke into the air. A flickering of light danced inside, a comforting sight, which meant warmth from the fire. Jim stopped dead and Brad came to a sudden halt.

"What?" Brad said.

"I don't know what your mother told you about the deer, but it was a miracle. Plain and simple. No one need believe me. Why should they? I'm dying. I need to hold onto strings. Well, the deer were not strings. They were real. I talked with them for hours. In the woods, tonight, I thought I saw one of them. That wasn't real. I was deluding myself."

He faced his son, who had let his arm fall, the flashlight illuminating the snow around them, touching on a bush nearby, and bringing the darkness of a tree trunk into the light, producing a smooth gray tone. The light fell onto their boots and onto their pant legs. Jim found himself staring at the light, thinking, not talking. What use was talking going to be? But this was his son; he needed to express how important the miracle had been, let Brad know that miracles were possible, maybe probable.

"The other deer, before," Jim said slowly, "the ones your mother told you about, they were real. You need to believe that. Know that. I'm not crazy or hallucinating. It's the truth."

"I know, Dad," Brad said. Then he flicked off the light. The ground, the snow, went gray, and the bush and tree, the pant legs and boots, all went black.

"I'll tell you about it." Jim wanted time, words, the right words to convince his son, but he didn't know if he had them. He'd try. Maybe in the accumulation of words, his own urgency, his own belief, would come through and touch Brad, too.

They walked back to the cabin. Jim talked on and on, trying to explain every detail. He talked around the subject just as Brad had explained Susan and he talked around love and sex. He wanted Brad to understand. He believed that in those details, if in nothing else, lay truth so clear it could not be disputed. He remembered how all the deer at the end of his visit appeared from nothing. When he got to that point in his explanation, he sighed. To him, it was still a miracle, still the most beautiful and awe-inspiring thing that had ever happened to him.

Brad listened closely the whole time, Jim could tell.

"Wow," Brad said at the end.

Jim felt rewarded for his story in that small exclamation.

"It was a real miracle," Jim said after a few moments of silence, of watching Brad slowly shake his head, almost in disbelief.

"It would be hard to make something like that up." Brad stood and walked near the fire, stood in its light and warmth while leaning against the mantel. The fire shed the only light in the room. "The details would be hard to memorize. They're the same details Mom told me. There's no reason for you to make anything up. You seem to believe what you're saying." Brad mumbled, trying to assess the validity of his father's story. He turned to face Jim, the fire at his back.

Jim looked up, but could not see into Brad's eyes.

Brad took a step closer. "If you told me you'd seen a shooting star, it'd be easy to believe you because I've seen them too. But I could only imagine the one you'd seen, not really see it. This is something I haven't seen, but I can imagine it too. It's just that every time I think of deer talking, it's like a cartoon, a Disney movie with animated deer. You're real," he added.

"Like Mary Poppins," Jim said.

Brad thought briefly of his childhood and shook his head, "Yes, like Mary Poppins with Dick Van Dyke in that amusement park dancing with penguins." Brad rubbed his cheek and scratched his ear, turning slowly to face the fire again. "This is more real than that, Dad. I've always just believed you. You never played any games with reality when we were little. Not like other parents who lied to their kids in fun. You were always completely honest. This is hard for me, but I believe you." Brad turned back to face his father. His voice cracked, "I never told you, but I believed that you talked with Connie after she died. I always believed you, no matter how much Mom didn't want me to. I don't know how I believe something this difficult to imagine, but I do. I've always thought that if a miracle could happen, it'd happen to you. You deserve it."

Brad covered his face with his hands. Recognizing Brad's movement for what it was, knowing what it meant, Jim felt touched, not so much because Brad believed in him, but because

Brad became so emotional over the situation that he'd cry. Jim let Brad place his face in his shoulder and cry for a moment. "I love you, Brad." Jim held his son.

Chapter 8

The next morning light fell through the bedroom window and woke the two of them almost simultaneously. Together they made coffee and breakfast, then took turns showering. When Brad came out of the shower, Jim had packed most of their gear for the trip home.

"We're leaving early?" Brad asked.

"No. I thought I'd try to pick up their trail. I just wanted to try one last time." He looked at his son for an answer to an unasked question.

"Sure, I'll go with you."

"Thank you. I'd love to have you along. I don't expect to find anything . . . "

"I know. I'd like to try with you, Dad."

"We'll head home after we're through," Jim said.

"Fine. I'm in no hurry. I just want to spend as much time with you as I can."

Jim smiled. The man who was once his son had become a long-time friend. Jim only wished he had found this friend sooner, but that wasn't the way it had happened. And after the miracle, Jim half-expected things to fall into place. He wasn't always sure he'd like the way things fell, but he was positive that they would fall.

Brad threw most of the gear into the trunk of the car. Jim dropped a bag onto the passenger seat and stuffed another one inside the game pouch of his hunting coat.

"What's that?" Brad wanted to know.

"What?"

"Those bags."

"Oh," Jim patted his pouch. "Lunch." Then pointed inside the car, "Snacks for the drive."

Brad laughed and started walking toward the woods.

"Wait." Jim ran to catch up and noticed how quickly he tired.

The morning grew into warmth like a fire's heat moves from paper to kindling to log. Overlooking the old farmhouse and barn, Brad commented on the barn's apparent lean to the south. He also noted, for the second time in two days, how the house looked occupied. "If it wasn't for how overgrown everything is."

"You're right," Jim agreed, "Even though the snows have lowered much of the growth, what is standing looks neglected."

"Maybe the barn, too, makes the whole place look neglected," Brad added.

Jim shook his head and walked on along the stone fence, again turning where several weeks earlier he had climbed over the stone and taken a path up through the woods.

This day a greater silence fell between the two men than the day before. Conversation had been given up to allow each man to explore the woods in his own way. An understanding had grown between them, allowing years of togetherness and respect to rush along behind them, to let them know each other as they never had. When Brad was a child, his father was in middle age. Brad now recognized that man. And Jim knew the boy Brad had been and the man he had become.

Through short bouts of conversation, they traveled over and around the obstacles of their lives that at one time Jim felt belonged to Becky and him alone. Finding now, that Brad had been there too, Jim wondered if he had paid any attention at all during those years. He owed it to his family and himself to believe in their plight if he expected them to believe in his.

The day wore on into lunch and sandwiches, and lighter conversation entered while they sat against a pine trunk in a small clearing. They roamed back and forth like a search party, looking for what they both intuitively knew they would not find. But, when twice they saw deer on their continued search after lunch, the look on Jim's face, the way his eyes probed for intimate recognition, further drove home Brad's acceptance of his father's miracle. Jim was driven by his encounter. It showed in his movements, his expressions, in his eyes. Brad had to believe. It had been the truth. Yet Jim had to carry the burden of experiencing the miracle only once. He had to live with his own doubt, a much heavier burden than the doubts of others.

After lunch, Jim tired more quickly. Eventually his resting

periods became almost as long as his walking periods.

Brad asked that they head home — back to the cabin, and then home.

"You had enough?" Jim asked.

"It's not that." Brad threw a bent stick he picked up at lunch to use as a walking stick. It flew, spinning into some brush a short distance from them.

"It is. You've become bored. I don't blame you. This was a wild goose chase. Even if they did show themselves again, they more than likely wouldn't do it with the two of us together."

"I'm not leaving you here alone." Brad anticipated Jim's next suggestion.

"No, I didn't mean that. I know Becky wouldn't allow me to come back here alone either. It's just over. I should accept that. Stop chasing rainbows," Jim said.

"Dad."

"No, it's true. I know it. God knows I know it's true. I've been thinking: here I am chasing a miracle down, trying to see it again, to feel it, when all along that's not what's important. It's not being in the experience as much as it is what you do with the experience afterwards. I've tried to figure out why the whole thing happened, but always through the muddle of chasing it down." Jim sat down after clearing snow from a small spot with his gloved hand. He looked up at his son, "You know, I used to look for deer to come out of that little strip of woods at the edge of the development. I'd take the long way to work in hopes of seeing the deer I met way up here somewhere along the highway. Waiting for me." He lowered and shook his head. "I don't know any of their names. I hardly remember what they said. I should have written it all down, but I was exhausted. I wasn't thinking."

"Dad, there's nothing to do. You said that Ed told you that you were a giver. He agreed with what the deer told you. Maybe that's it. I think you are too. Christ, I know you've had problems with Mom, but you've never given up. Not as long as I've known you."

"I did once."

"Once. Mom used to ignore you for days when you disagreed with her. And you're worried about once. Besides, Connie used to be there for you. She took up the slack when Mom couldn't. When she was gone . . ."

"But the deer," Jim said, almost in tears. Then he lifted his face. "The one deer, the buck, said something about remembering that I was a part of everything, forever. It said forever," he repeated. "Like Connie. That's how she could be there, she always would be. It's the deer again." Jim stood and stared past Brad.

Brad thought that his father was making a true statement, that it was the deer again, standing behind him. Brad turned to look, but there was nothing there. For an instant he felt disbelief in the miracle. If Jim was seeing deer and he was not, it seemed logical that . . .

Jim spoke, "No, they're not there. What I mean is the word: *deer*. Get it?"

Brad cocked his head like a curious animal.

"Singular and plural. *Deer*. Individual and universal. Connie, me, everyone. We're all here, forever," Jim explained.

Brad shook his head in affirmation, but made no attempt to speak.

"The voices," Jim said. "When the deer appeared in the forest, all around, they said, one said—no, more than one—a whisper made loud by numbers, one and many. Get it? They said, 'Become, *Giver*,' like an order. What more can I do?" He looked to his son for an answer that wasn't there. "The question's for me to answer. It wasn't directed at you. I'll have to figure it out myself. And I will," Jim promised. "And when I know what it is, if it's any greater than what I have already come to, I'll tell you."

Brad stood still, listening to his father go on about the deer. Jim went over the story again, a more excited, but shorter, version.

"I just have to learn to be," Jim said, "that's all. To become. Even if I don't know what that means. Even if I never know."

"You are, Dad. You always have been and you always will be, for me, Mom, Connie, even Susan now. You've been around for my whole life; you're a part of it all. What more can you be? What more is there?"

For a time, Jim was satisfied with that. "What more can you be?" Brad had said. And it was an excellent question. Even so, Jim wanted there to be more. At least with Becky and him. On the way back to the cabin, Jim planned a reunion with her. In his mind it went well, perfectly, even though he knew that wouldn't be the case.

Before dropping Brad off at his house, Jim turned and thanked him for taking the trip.

"You don't need to thank me, Dad. I wanted to go. I'm sorry we didn't do it earlier."

"Me, too, but it's done now."

"No, it's started. If you need to talk with someone, I'd like to be that person. I can learn a lot from you. I'm willing to. Don't make it too late."

Neither had mentioned Jim's cancer the whole trip. The only times they came close were moments like this.

"The deer told me to hold on. I remember that, too. Now. The words. 'Hold on,' they said."

"Then hold on, Dad. Do it for them, for us, for you, but hold on."

Chapter 9

The next few weeks, every time Jim tried to get close to Becky it didn't work out. She'd hold him or kiss him, but only as a long-time married partner, not as a new-found lover. Then, after a few more treatments, came the news that the cancer was in remission. When Becky found out, she kissed him with such sensual aggression that Jim felt the old spark inside himself. Just one kiss opened new doors.

Becky organized a party. Everyone knew about the remission anyway. It seemed odd, but Jim wanted to share the news formally. "It'll be a reason to bring everyone together. Personally, I think that's a good reason."

"We don't want people coming out of pity, though."

"We'll only invite those who would come no matter what,"

Jim said.

"Good idea," Susan confirmed — it was her interest that swayed them — "close friends and family."

It was settled.

That Saturday Mel and Ed and their wives visited Jim, Becky, Brad, and Susan. Some friends of Becky's showed up too. While Becky and Susan prepared food and punch for ten people, Jim and Brad made remission posters: Welcome Remission, The Joy of Remission, For Whom The Remission Tolls.

The house grew loud with a crowd of people in the living room eating food and drinking beer. Jim had tuned in an easy-listening station on the radio. The announcer's voice added to the confusion of voices in the room. The party rode along gaily, reminiscent of past Christmas or New Year's parties. Until, that is, Mel asked Jim to speak. "Speech!" he yelled.

Ed chimed in, too. "Speech!"

Eventually the room quieted and the small group separated to give Jim the floor. He didn't know what to say. In a way, he wanted to cry. Suddenly, he felt as though the party were a sham. How long did he expect to stay in remission? It was a death party and he had nothing to give, no insight, no profound statement. Nothing.

Pushed by an invisible, yet overwhelming force, Jim stepped into the middle of the room. He turned until he could see everyone, then backed up. The evening was nearly over. Some of them had had too much to drink. Could they even hear what he said? Could any of them understand how he felt, even if he could explain it? Probably not. So, what was there to say? "I . . ." He lowered his head. "You all know me. There's nothing to say that you don't know."

"How do you feel?" Ed asked.

"Blessed." That was an easy question to answer.

"Does the remission give you a new lease on life?" Mel offered.

Jim thought for a moment. The people stood still and quiet. All eyes were on him. Out the window, darkness had fallen so close to the house that the windows looked painted over. He wanted to turn off the lights, to open up the outside world once again. *The magic of physics,* he thought. Then, he checked himself. His mind had wandered. He felt nervous. What did they want from him?

"Come on, Jim. Just say something." Becky's voice sounded cruel, as though he was purposely stalling, but he wasn't.

"Okay, fine, I feel more than blessed. I have for a while. Ever since the deer. You all know about them, I'm sure." He looked accusingly at them all. Some heads turned away. He noticed that Brad's did not. Brad actually stood taller.

"What deer?" Bob, the husband of one of Becky's friends, asked.

"Shush," his wife scolded.

"I talked with deer," Jim said.

"Oh, good God." Becky left the circle, and Jim saw someone reach for her hand to comfort her.

"It doesn't matter. It was a miracle. No one has to believe me. Not any more. But I'm not crazy. It happened, and some day, I believe a miracle will happen to each of you, even if it's only moments before you die. That's when you'll believe."

"The deer said that we're all part of everything," he continued speaking straight from his thoughts, no translations. "Here," he reached out and touched Bob's hand, "I've touched your life, not just physically, but now that way too. It's there forever. It's permanent. You can't change it. I'm part of everything I touch. So are you. The deer said that and more. We're all, each of us, individual and universal. If you love someone, that love goes everywhere, whether you like it or not. In fact, everything you do is everywhere."

"Karma," Bob said.

"He understands. Yes. More than I do, I think." Jim pointed at Bob. "Listen to him. He knows." Jim turned and touched Ed, then Ed's wife, Joan. "That's why we must touch one another, to touch the individual and the all. We're all responsible for everyone else through our individual actions. In teaching, I teach you all. Don't you see?"

"I do," Brad said. But Jim knew Brad had seen long before that moment.

Others shook their heads. It didn't seem that the deer were any longer important. It wasn't where or how he got the information, it was the information itself that mattered. Even Becky came back into the circle.

Jim took her hand, "Our love and our understanding. We, working through our personal problems, have touched each of you, know it or not. The fact that we've overcome some of those problems has taught a great lesson to each of you, and to everyone else in this world, even if the message is different for each." He pulled Becky to him and slid his arm around her waist. Then he reached out and touched Ed, who stood closest to him. "We should all touch more often, look at each other more often, explore our lives, not just live them."

"That's good," Bob said. "Explore our lives." He was a little drunk and slurred, which brought some laughter, and the laughter broke up the seriousness of Jim's short speech.

"We'll explore, all right," Mel said, and soon others began to talk.

Jim pulled back into the circle as the center closed up. In an hour, everyone had talked and drunk and eaten until they became tired. Each thanked Jim at least once before leaving. At the final door closing, Becky stood facing him. "That wasn't so bad," she said, but her face said more. She looked proud.

"The deer thing?" he asked.

"You're a brave man. I think you're braver than I've ever known you to be, and I've lived with you all these years. I think it's just that you never had an occasion to be brave until recently. That's a shame."

Jim took the opportunity to reach for her. They hugged for a long time, out of love, out of tiredness, out of mutual respect. He rubbed his hands up and down her back, along her sides. Becky laid her head on his shoulder, as he remembered her doing many years before. The lights dimmed as he closed his eyes and held her. The two of them were suspended there; he hoped it could be forever, but Becky moved away. Just before she lifted her head, Jim felt the tension in her return.

"We need to clean up," she said.

"It can wait." Jim wanted another moment. "I'll do it later." He reached for her again.

"I'm proud of you, Honey," she said as though that was all she could do. He had to take that for now.

"Thank you." He turned away for a moment, then turned back. She was leaning over the coffee table picking up dirty dishes. Jim came up behind her and touched the small of her back.

Becky stood with a stack of plates in her hands. She looked into his eyes, not without compassion. "I'm fifty-eight. I'm an old woman, not a young lover. What is it that you need from me?"

"Do you love me?" he asked.

"I wouldn't be here if . . ."

"Young love? Do you love me like you used to?"

Holding the dishes in front of her, she stepped past him. "I'm not young. But I still love you. Yes. More than you love me, I believe." She was in the kitchen by the time she finished the sentence.

He followed behind her. "Then hold me again. I don't want you to love me from a distance. I want you near me."

"It'll never be the same," she said.

"Then let's make it completely different," he said.

She shook her head. "You are brave to be saying this to an old—"

"Lady whom I've just met for the first time. There are some tiny things about you that remind me of someone I love very much. But there are also new things I need to explore." He walked up to her and wrapped his arms around her waist. He kissed her lightly, then wiggled his lips to get her to part hers. They kissed like a young couple. Becky breathed through her nose to get air. Jim pulled her hips closer to his own. "I do love you," he whispered into her ear once he let her lips go.

"Oh, why has it taken this…this…so long." Becky tried to speak, but couldn't come up with enough words, or the right words.

Jim led her into the living room, holding her hand. He turned off the living room light. The front lawn, suffused with light from a streetlamp down the block, cast a soft whiteness into the darkened room. Jim began to unbutton Becky's blouse.

"What are you doing?"

"Take off your clothes," he said.

"What?" She whispered as though someone might be listening.

"Take off your clothes."

"Jim! I'm an old woman."

"You're my wife, my lover. Please." He removed his own pants and shorts and shoes. He stood in only a shirt. When he bent to begin to unbutton her buttons again, she leaned in to kiss him. A sensation of newness rushed through him. He thought he could feel it in her also.

Her hands quickly rushed to her belt to loosen it, then to help with the buttons. Once her clothes were on the floor, Jim unhooked her bra and let her heavy breasts fall loose. She grabbed for them with her hands, to hold them up. "Oh, Honey, I sag everywhere." She stood there in only pantyhose.

Jim removed her hands and placed his over her breasts, holding them up.

"I can't," she said.

He pulled her close and kissed her again.

"No." She pushed him away. "I'm not a teenager. This isn't high school." Becky bent down to collect her clothes, then walked into the bedroom, leaving Jim standing alone in the darkness.

Jim watched. From behind she could have been twenty years younger. Even from the front, he thought. He looked down and noticed he was hard. He wanted to make love with her, but even more to sit with her. He wanted to explore her body like he hadn't done in years. Touch places he'd ignored, rediscover places he thought he knew well. These included her thoughts, too. He wanted to exchange thoughts and emotions.

A car drove by. Jim watched the lights reflect off the remaining snow. Spring was around the corner. How long would his new life last? "Speak to me again, Connie. Now, when I need your help." Jim held out his hands as he had once when Connie would visit him. But she had not visited for a long while. He had eventually told her she could go on. He no longer needed to hold her back. He felt differently now. Tears swelled in his eyes and he began to shake. He felt something in the room with him; the way he used to feel when they talked. But this time she didn't talk. "Please," he whispered. He felt alone.

The wind bent the trees out front. Snow blew along the ground.

He let his arms drop back to his sides. On the sofa, Jim buried his face into his hands and sobbed quietly. "Be," he said. "Be what? Miserable? Alone?" He waited for a little while, not so much for an answer, but for his feelings of loneliness to subside. When they didn't, he got up from the couch. Even if things weren't going well, at least Becky tried. And she said that she loved him. She called him brave. There was no reason to give up, only to give her time.

Jim collected his clothes and walked into the bedroom. They still shared a bed. Many people he'd met had stopped doing that for one excuse or another. He removed his shirt and climbed in beside her.

"I'm sorry I'm not as brave as you," Becky said.

Jim didn't expect her to talk at all. He thought it was over. "I was scared as hell. I just needed to connect again. To talk."

"Is that what you wanted?"

"Brad told me about Susan and him. I wanted us to sit, facing each other, naked. To look at each other. To fall back in love."

Becky rolled over to face him. "That's a tall order."

"We owe it to ourselves. To each other. God knows I owe you much more than that," he said.

"I just can't. I'm old. I'm sagging."

"It's not your skin I'm in love with," Jim whispered.

"But." She couldn't think of any other words.

Neither could he.

"Hold me," she said, desperation in her voice.

Jim slid to her and stuffed his arm under her body. Her breasts fell together and in the dim light Jim could see the long heavy-shadowed line of her cleavage. He kissed her forehead and held her until she fell off to sleep. Then, he lay on his back and stared, for several hours, at the ceiling. Even he didn't know what he had wanted, what he had expected.

He slept lightly, dreaming that Connie had come to talk with him. He woke early Sunday morning.

Becky was sound asleep on the opposite side of the bed, the blanket tucked under her arm and her broad back spreading upward. Her skin was smooth, her hair delicate.

Jim started to reach for her then pulled back. *Why wake her?* He slipped out of bed and collected his clothes for the day. Without showering or shaving, and carrying a bundle of clothes in his arms, he went into the kitchen to make coffee. He dressed, sitting in a cold kitchen chair, while the coffee dripped. He filled a

Styrofoam cup to the brim with a strong, black brew, put on a coat, and stepped outside into the yard.

The snow crunched under his feet. The sky was clear. Birds chirped overhead in the few trees that stood in the yard.

Jim breathed deeply. He wanted to go over a few things, particularly the night before, with a clear head. He stopped long enough to take a good sip of the coffee and felt it warm his throat and chest. Then, carefully, he walked down to the sidewalk and up the street. First of all, Connie was not coming back, nor should she. He must let that connection go. The same for the deer—let them go, too. Remember them and her. That's what was left. If he needed to talk, he'd talk with Brad. Brad had asked to be the one. Or he'd talk with Becky, if that were possible.

Jim took in the cool air while stopping occasionally to sip his coffee. The sun rose above the houses and the birds cried, "Spring, spring, spring," all around him. Nothing seemed impossible; nothing seemed too far away to grasp. He felt strong and capable. He had his friends, his family, and his memories. Things came to him clearly: his place in the world, his individual and universal significance. But the understanding didn't enter with words he could repeat. He just knew. Felt. Was. Maybe that was what was meant by *be*.

He recalled the magical light in the forest and transferred it to the glimmer of sun off snow where he now walked. The deer had come as friends, friends from another world, maybe the spirit world where Connie now lived. Yet deer are more connected to the Earth and therefore operate on this plane, and it seemed right. All his thoughts seemed right that morning, but he'd talk with Brad about it, and maybe Becky, too.

The morning washed away like an outgoing tide, while Jim walked. The coffee gone and the sun warming the air, he turned down the street, which, through his circuitous walk, would take him home again. The rhythm of nature, from seed to tree to seed, from birth to death, and maybe to birth again; or from morning to night, always he came back home, no matter how many times around the block, or the neighborhood. Jim placed his hand on the door knob and smelled bacon. His mind shot back to the farmhouse, to the farmer and his wife. He first thought of their romance and the romance of their way of life—what Brad had seen about them. But then, he remembered the hollowness of the house without them and remembered his own hollowness. In one moment, his heart ached for what he did not have, and for what would not be missing in his house when he died…the romance.

Chapter 10

In a few months, the cancer came out of remission. Spring was running full speed ahead. The neighborhood became more lush day by day, and warm evening air carried the voices of children.

Jim tried several times to approach Becky on an intimate level, suggesting they sit on the floor naked, to talk and explore, but Becky couldn't do it. She still didn't see the purpose in exploiting their old bodies while trying to bring back young love. The last time he attempted to approach her, she saw it coming and actually left the house. So, they carried on their relationship as they always had: comfortable, caring, and sexual at times. Becky still thought him brave for "sticking to his guns."

The miracle of the deer had become an element of conversation, and the relaxed atmosphere about it allowed Jim to remember more, most of which, by this time, he kept to himself. In fact, in opposite proportion to the relaxed atmosphere, he became increasingly secretive for fear of losing the mystery. An odd thought at first, but as time went on, it proved an accurate one. With all the other people involved in the mystery of the deer's words, there also came too many answers, and from too many directions. Jim felt removed from his own experience. He knew that it had happened to him, and extrapolated from that that it was also meant for him. As much as he appreciated their thoughts, his friends and family plagued him with answers, none of which were his own. Their well-intentioned help physically exhausted him.

"It's the chemo too, Dad," Brad said one day when Jim was complaining adamantly.

Jim took the coffee mug from Brad's hands. "Thank you."

"How'd it go today?" Brad asked.

"Who knows? I think they stop telling you the truth once you're heading down the opposite side of the mountain."

"That's not true," Becky said from the kitchen doorway. "He just wants to believe that it is."

"So, what'd they say?" Brad asked her.

"They have it under control," Becky told him.

"But it's in my body," Jim said.

"Take it easy, Dad. They're doing all they can."

"Yeah, yeah, I know."

"He gets like this sometimes," Becky said. "Depressed. God knows, I'd be worse in his situation. Most of the time, it's like he doesn't even think of it."

"Oh, I think of it, I just try not to. And I don't talk about it," Jim said.

"Even while you're getting sick after the treatments?" Brad said.

"I focus on the deer. On my interpretation, not everyone else's, and let it happen. I just let everything happen. It's all I can do now." He sipped his coffee. "Your mother's here to help me get through it."

Brad looked up at Becky.

"It's not always easy for me," she said.

"It's probably worse for you than me," Jim admitted. "I know how I feel; you can only guess. That's got to be tough."

They all sat quietly for a minute.

Finally Jim spoke again. "That's why I want you to go with me."

"Take Brad," Becky suggested.

"Where?" Brad wanted to know.

"No!" Jim slammed his fist against the chair arm. Coffee leaped from the cup, but did not spill onto the chair.

"Where's he want to go?" Brad asked.

"To that old farm," Becky told him, "but I'm no outdoorsman. I can't walk through the mountains."

"Then I'll go alone. I just wanted you there, that's all." Jim said.

"It's not a difficult walk, Mom."

"Listen to your son. He knows," Jim said.

"Why should I go look at a run-down farm?"

"You don't have to. I'll go alone. I want to see it. I just wanted you with me. But it's me who needs to go. It reminds me of myself," Jim told them both.

"Run-down?" Becky said. "That's not you."

"Empty. Full of dead romance. The memory of usefulness," he said.

"Go, Mom."

Becky shook her head and walked over to Jim. She put her hand on his shoulder. "I've never in my life met anyone like you."

"You're lucky if you never do again."

"It hasn't been easy."

"Something must be okay. You're still together."

Both his parents shot him a look, both saying that he didn't know the whole truth of the matter.

"Sorry." Brad patted Jim on the knee and stood up. "Look, I've got to go. Susan's expecting me home early today. She has some sort of plans." Neither one of them appeared to be listening to him. Jim had all but closed his eyes and Becky seemed off in another world.

"I'll leave you two alone," he said, as if they were going to spend quality time together. He could hope so.

Jim's eyes widened. "You don't have to go."

"Susan's waiting."

"So you said," Jim said.

Brad kissed Becky's cheek. "For what it's worth, Mom, I think you should go."

Jim thanked Brad, knowing that Becky would be more likely to listen to her son than she would to him. He didn't blame her. Through the expanse of their life together, they had both let the relationship grow into what it was. And, at the moment, he felt much too tired to try to change it. Her hand on his shoulder, its warmth and feel, belied his thoughts on what they had become. Sometimes, it seemed there were more elements to their marriage than even he could understand. He felt her lean over and kiss his neck; her breath, the odor of morning coffee, lingered there. She slipped the cup from his hands, her fingers brushing against his. Then he heard her footsteps as she walked away and he drifted into a light sleep.

Chapter 11

If she was going to go on the trip at all, it was going to be that weekend. "Or I might change my mind completely," she said.

"It might rain again," he said.

"Then we'll take an umbrella."

"Fine, just fine."

"I thought you wanted to go see this…thing that reminds you of yourself. This old farm."

"You don't have to be so derogatory. And yes, I do want to go. I was just hoping for some better weather." He remembered how the sun hit the house and the field, the snow on the ground. There wouldn't be snow, but the field illuminated by sun would be much more beautiful than drenched with rain. He got up and walked past

Becky toward the bedroom.

He wanted to be alone for a moment. They had spent the last few days cooped up in the house because of the rain. "I need to change my shirt," he said. "The collar's bothering me." He continued to talk until he entered the haven of the bedroom. He didn't want to hear it, not any more. She had become more aggressive as he became more tired. It seemed to him that she was badgering, picking a little at a time, eating away at him. Even though she was willing to go on the trip with him, she picked. That was her scheme: look like you're doing the right thing, like you're going along, but undermine the whole operation by nit-picking, whining, and complaining. That way it's ruined for both of them.

Jim took off his shirt, but it took him a while to choose another one. After all, it didn't matter what he wore, he was going nowhere but to the grave, and he didn't need clothes for that one. He reached behind his back to scratch. His skin had become so dry and itchy lately. He had neck aches and headaches too. He tried to read while he was home, but his eyes had become light sensitive, burning if there was too much light or too little. His whole body had turned on him, had begun to rebel against him. *Fifty-eight was not old enough to have such problems. Maybe an occasional backache or tight joint, but not all this*. He scratched for a little while then pulled a shirt from the closet. When he turned, Becky was there standing quietly, watching him.

"Let me put some lotion on your back." Her voice sounded calm and loving.

Jim couldn't refuse, so he turned back around.

Becky had brought lotion with her and began to cover his back and sides. "I love you," she said. "I don't mean to be so irritable. I guess I'm trying not to miss you when I know I will."

Jim heard her voice crack and turned in time for his shoulder to catch her lowering head and the tears that dripped from her eyes. He put his arms around her, placing his hands near the soft flesh of her neck. "Oh, Honey, don't be afraid. It'll all happen just as it's supposed to."

"How can you say that?" she mumbled into his shoulder.

He thought about her question. "There's nothing else to say."

"You worry. I know you do. You can't hide it all the time."

"I don't worry. At least it doesn't feel like worry. Maybe sadness, a slight depression, but worry? No. I know I have no choice in the matter. What's happening is natural. The destructive aspect of nature. It's stronger than I am. It's stronger than all mankind. All these months I have tried to be one with it. That's not always easy. Sometimes I just want to be alive longer, but I'm not there, not in the future, and I know it." Jim laughed softly. "It's funny, in a way, not seeing yourself in the future. But it's all part of being, physical or not."

"Honey…"

"No, Beck, I'm serious here. I feel strongly that I'll always be part of the whole, forever and ever. I haven't lost that. Remember? Deer. It's both individual and multiple. Intimate and universal. That's what I've come to believe. So, now I understand the word *sheep*, too, as in the Bible, maybe. We are His herd. I don't claim to know, or to be that religious. It's just what I've explored."

"You're allowed, Jimmy. You don't have to apologize."

"I don't mean to talk so much." He squeezed her close to him. "It might just be a reason to hold you longer."

"Oh, you." She held him close, her bare hands, softened by the lotion, rubbed his equally softened back.

"I love you, Rebecca. And I love the beautiful children we raised, and the life we lived. Most of it."

"Don't," she said.

"Don't what?"

"Don't throw part of your life away. I've forgiven you. I really have," she promised.

"But every time I try to . . ."

"You're asking a lot of an old woman. I'm embarrassed. In fact, some of the things you've suggested, I would have been embarrassed about when I was younger and more adventuresome."

They kissed comfortably.

"We'll make the trip," Jim said. "Rain or no rain. We'll leave tomorrow evening, sleep over and hike out Saturday morning."

"Good. I really want to see this place now." She sounded like she meant it.

"I'm glad I finally explored it. Even if it took the cancer to make it important," Jim said.

"Brad told me how important this is to you. We've talked about it a lot lately."

"What is he, a double agent?" Jim smiled.

"No. But you two have spent a lot of time together since your trip there. Some of it's bound to come out."

Jim didn't mind. He had actually almost hoped that Brad and Becky would talk even more after he died. In a way, he wanted to be remembered. What he and Brad explored together, in his heart, was very spiritual, very enlightening. Jim was often amazed at the things he'd taught Brad without realizing it, like "Eat healthy, think healthy." He'd forgotten he used to say that when Brad and

Connie were kids. Now, Brad repeated it back to Jim.

Jim kissed Becky again, on the forehead. "I'm glad you two talk."

"So am I. He's so much like you. I never noticed until lately," she said.

"Since you've been talking?" Jim let go of Becky and put his shirt on. The tension of their earlier confrontation in the living room had dispersed into another kind of conversation, one of mutual understanding.

"No," she said, "since I've paid more attention to you. I'd lost track of just how intelligent and introspective you are, questioning everything. I remember times in our life together when I was irritated to no end that you questioned so heavily and deeply, not only me but yourself. You'd get into depressions for days. Then, you'd just snap out of it." She snapped her fingers and raised her eyes to illustrate. "You wouldn't have an answer though, not in words, but you'd have a solution. It drove me crazy sometimes."

She went over and helped him button his shirt and roll the sleeves evenly. "Hearing Brad ask all those questions about himself reminds me of you. I appreciate it much more now, how important it is to his well-being." She again threw her arms around him. "He is so lucky to have found Susan to share his life with. She's just like him. They have a wonderful relationship."

"They do, don't they?"

"I'm sorry you were saddled with me all those years, my misunderstanding your quietness and rejecting your way of living with yourself and the world."

"I wasn't saddled."

"Sometimes?" she asked.

"I was well taken care of."

They stood together for a long time. An understanding came between them, spawned by a closeness of spirit. The rest of the afternoon and evening their conversation consisted of memories of their life together. Without remorse, they spoke of Connie and of Jim's condition. They connected on a deep level realized through calm, deeply felt emotions, and caring spirits. When the conversation turned to the deer, Jim felt an intimacy with them he had not felt for a long time. Becky did not try to translate their words or the incident, instead she asked probing questions of Jim, what he remembered, how he felt then, and now. Still, it had all become memory, sifted through the thin screen of time into a soft powder. It was the physicality of the deer themselves that was the message; the fact that *they* were there, not their words so much. And also, the fantasy they wrapped themselves in, or that he wrapped them in. So, they were a gift, one he had unwrapped slowly, all these months. And like every child must learn eventually, it is the act of the gift given, and the gift giver, that is most important, not what is inside the wrappings.

By Friday evening, the two of them were excited and ready for the trip into the mountains. As soon as they loaded the car, they were off. Becky drove, all the while acting like a young bride going on her honeymoon. It made Jim giddy and nervous, but anxious too.

"Look there," Becky stretched her arm in front of him. Two deer grazed near a stand of pale-stemmed birches. "Maybe it's an omen."

"An omen?"

"That you'll get to see *your* deer again."

"I doubt that, but you never know. I'd prefer we called it a sign though. Omen sounds evil or something," Jim said.

"Occult," Becky added.

"Maybe they're just beautiful," Jim said, as he squeezed her shoulder.

Becky drove more slowly than Brad, so they were not making very good time. She apologized, but Jim told her they were on a pleasure trip so arrival time was much less important than together time. She agreed and suggested, in that case, they stop along the way for dinner instead of making something once they got to the cabin.

"Great idea." Jim remembered the area fairly well, having traveled it so often. "There's a place I've been interested in trying, but never have. It's about thirty minutes up the road here."

"Then, let's do it," Becky said.

Jim reached over and patted Becky's thigh and let his hand rest there for a moment. Slowly, he inched it up to her breast and jiggled it a little.

"I don't know what's gotten into you, but if it doesn't stop we're going straight to the cabin and you're getting no dinner," she told him.

"I didn't want to stop anywhere anyway."

Becky gave him a peck on the cheek and got back to her driving. They talked about how beautiful the drive had been thus far.

"I forget sometimes that you've never been here," Jim said.

"I'm sorry, now. It's just that it's your hunting retreat. I always thought you wanted your own place to go."

"I think I did in a way. But, you know, we could have come up here in the spring or summer sometimes, so you could have enjoyed it too," he said.

"Well, let's make this our first time — it is — and a special time." She smiled over at him.

"The diner's around the bend up here," he pointed through the window.

"I am a little hungry," she said.

"Me too, really. Do you think it matters how much fat and cholesterol I have now? I'd really like some fried food."

Becky reacted unpleasantly to his allusion by not answering. She glanced over at him, not smiling, not saying a word as she pulled into the parking lot. "You've always eaten any way you like," she snapped. "Why stop now?" Her words had a familiar curtness about them, yet she took his arm and bumped his hip with hers in a most unfamiliar way as they walked through the parking lot. She held a tight smile on her face, playful and serious at once.

The gravel scrunched beneath their feet. *Crowder Mt. Café* the sign over the door proclaimed. A waitress ushered them to a booth. Jim sat next to Becky and pushed her closer to the wall with his butt.

"What in the world?" Becky asked.

"I'm sitting with you for a change," he winked. "You started it and I like feeling your legs against mine."

"I think you don't want to look at me," she teased.

"Not so, it's the vantage point from which I look. I've changed it."

"You certainly have."

They ordered, Jim finding fried catfish and French fries to his liking.

"You're going to feel awful later," Becky warned.

"But it'll taste good now."

Becky ordered chicken stir-fry and a small dinner salad. "They probably fry the lettuce in a place like this anyway."

"Beck, have you ever wondered what my purpose in your life has been?" She looked away and Jim noticed a slight sniffle. "Are you all right?"

"Yes." She looked back at him. He loved her smooth cheeks and the bone structure around her eyes. They hadn't changed much in all that time, only aged, and slowly, elegantly. Had he ever expressed these thoughts clearly enough? After many years with Rebecca, he expected her to know how he felt about her and how he viewed her, physically. At that moment, he knew he must tell her more often. Similarly, he had always known there was a sort of mystery to life, to the world, but it took his actual encounter with the deer for him to make it a part of him. "I love the way you look, how smooth your cheeks feel when they brush against mine."

Ignoring his statement, she answered his question. "I've often wondered about us, in many ways, at every stage of life. I know I'm not as introspective as you are, but, in my own way, I evaluate our life together. You are always the mystery in life to me. I often don't know what you're thinking or how you're feeling exactly. Your moods change and I'm on a bumpy country road beside you wondering just how you feel inside about me, about yourself, about the cancer." She choked then coughed into her hand.

"You don't have to go on," Jim said, patting her leg.

"No, I want to." She put the napkin to her face and dabbed her eyes.

The waitress returned with their drinks. She obviously noticed

Becky, but made no comment. After she left, Becky continued. "Your mind flits about like a dozen small birds in the bushes: you see their flight, their quick movements, but never quite get a clear look at them. But they're beautiful, quick, and alive. You are, and always have been, very much alive to me. You always will be."

She placed her head on his shoulder and he could feel her will herself to stop crying. Had they been in a different setting, she'd have let herself break down completely, and he would have held her until she stopped. This was a conversation for later, when both of them could feel free to speak out or cry if they wanted.

They made the meal their focus. They spoke very little, and only then to comment on the food. Jim felt his emotions rise and fall during dinner. Every time Becky and he touched, his heart raced. When she purposely pushed her leg against his, he almost burst into tearful joy. They acted like children, teenagers on a date. After eating, they held hands as they drank coffee. Again, they spoke very little, both afraid what might, or might not, be said. When the waitress brought the check, Jim asked her to wait, and paid the bill right away, so they could leave, quickly.

Once back on the road, this time with Jim driving, Becky broke down. Jim reached over and she grasped his hand with both of hers and wept into it. He could feel her tears and her shivering. "It'll be okay," he said. "It'll be fine."

"It won't." She held his hand to her cheek. "I know what's happening. You're making a last pilgrimage, and you're taking me as a witness. You've given up."

"No. You're wrong there. I haven't given up. I've accepted. There's a difference. For some reason, once I got to a certain point in all this, it dawned on me that my time here has always been limited. I always knew I was going to die. We all know it. I just didn't know when. As I get closer, it gets easier to take. I feel lucky, really."

"Lucky?" Her face lifted to reveal incredulity.

"I've had a lot of time to think, to get to know my son, to get closer to you. That, I think is my greatest gift." He noticed the confused expression on her face, so he went on. "If I had lived another ten or twenty years, without the cancer, I would not have changed a thing. Our relationship would have deteriorated, and Brad and I would still be separated by decades of parenting. These last months have been a gift. They've allowed me to repair things. If I had had a heart attack, it'd be all over. No time to think. Plenty of regrets on all sides."

"Then you've given us the greatest gift, too." Her tears were gone. "You've allowed us to know you better, you have penetrated deeper into our lives. I will never forget you, how brave you are, how caring." Becky removed a tissue from the glove box and wiped tears from the back of Jim's hand, then from her own eyes.

"Living takes brave people. We're all heroes, gift givers," Jim said.

Becky reached out and touched his cheek.

Chapter 12

The next morning Jim got up early to make coffee and get ready for their trip. Becky rose more slowly. When she came out of the bedroom Jim was sitting on the couch watching the fire. "What are you doing?" she asked.

Jim held up his coffee cup. "Relaxing." He turned to face her. Her robe was open and he could see the soft flesh of her cleavage, her slightly pudgy stomach and, where her pubic area should have been, she had one leg pushed forward. From head to foot he could see inviting flesh. The robe, like a door standing ajar, let out the light of her body.

"What's it like outside," she asked him.

"Drizzling. Overcast," he said.

"I was hoping it would have stopped."

"Me to. I hate to scrap this whole thing, but you won't . . . "

"Don't tell me what I won't do or won't like. I'm going through with this. It's too important not to," she said.

"It's important to me," he told her.

"And therefore important to me."

Her confidence and sense of mission was attractive. He got up from the couch and walked over to her. He ran his hand down the front of her body.

"But there's no reason we have to go right away," she said.

Jim took her hand and led her back into the bedroom.

Their love, for years, had become comfortable and familiar. The two of them knew what to expect, one from the other, and knew what to give. The pleasures of knowing one another well and caring about their feelings had led to a satisfying love life where warmth and understanding and acceptance were all given with honesty.

Later, when they were both ready for the hike, Becky pulled Jim close and held him. "Thank you," she said, but she didn't have to.

The rain added substance to the odor of the woods. A lingering of smoke in the air brushed by, making the outside familiar. Jim had smelled those smells a lot lately and welcomed them into his body. He would miss the land as much as he'd miss anything, he thought.

Becky grabbed his hand and asked, "Which way?"

"Was I lingering too long?" he said.

"You were thinking. It's okay."

Jim led her to the path, which took them up to the ridge that led around the hill. From the ridge, in brighter light, Jim knew the farmhouse would rise gloriously from the golden field. He hoped that, even in the rain, it would give life to the valley. If he needed anything from the old farm now, it was life… just as his was fading. He needed to know that some things lasted, just as the love inside that farmhouse had outlasted the two people who once shared it.

Becky had some trouble with the hike, stumbling over fallen branches and underbrush, but Jim held tightly to her hand and helped her keep steady.

"I'm a little old for this sort of thing," she complained. "I'm used to sidewalks and malls."

"It's only a little farther. Can you make it?"

His concern made her want to make it. She knew that, ultimately, if she said no, he'd turn back. For her. She couldn't do that to him. She stumbled, again, and Jim turned in time to catch her before her knees hit the ground. "I'm sorry, Honey," he said, "let's turn back. I'll come back later, alone."

"No." She straightened her clothes and pulled at her jacket to unfluff the front of it. Her hair was damp and sagging. She hadn't put makeup on that morning and her face looked pale and uneven. She was beginning to look a wreck. The dense woodsy odor followed her, and when she spoke, her breath smelled of the earth.

Jim held her up for a moment while she straightened herself out. His stare brought out her question, "What is it?"

"Nothing," he said. "You look like you belong here."

"In the woods?"

"Yes."

"I don't feel that way," she huffed.

"But you look it."

She smiled at him. "You and your woods. What is it about them?"

"They're true. Nothing can change them, alter them, if they're left alone." He thought for a moment. "Nature, all of it, it seems to me, is the deep truth of us—how we are. That probably sounds stupid."

"Not at all."

"If we're reflected in our jobs, then why not in nature?" He shook his hand in the air to illustrate everything around them. "It's all just a manifestation of what we are. How we feel and think. To me, nature is part of us."

"It's part of you, I know that much." Becky knew that for all the time they had been together; she had listened and watched him enough to know how he felt about nature.

She tugged at his arm, "Let's go. I'm getting cold and wet."

The drizzle had picked up. Tiny droplets of moisture trickled down the sides of Jim's cheeks. He held close to Becky to keep her upright. He could tell she was tiring. He smelled the air, inhaling deeply, felt the moisture on his skin. His chest swelled with emotion. He wanted to reach the farmhouse soon. He wanted to touch its door, the stair railing. He wondered if it'd look occupied or empty as they approached. And the barn? He felt so much at home there. "Almost there," he said. "If it were sunny, we'd probably be able to see it through the trees." He had gone into the woods a little further than he would normally have gone, trying to keep the light rain from drenching them any more than it had. The mist seemed to rise from the ground as well as fall from the sky, making their attempts to keep dry unsuccessful.

He pointed into the trees. "Through there." He could see nothing but mist and fog beyond the green. Becky didn't seem impressed or anxious. "Can you make it straight down the hill?"

"I'll try."

Jim helped her, so conscious of her progress that he almost slipped once himself, taking her with him. When the field finally opened up, his back was to it because he was still helping Becky down the hill. When the decline leveled off, he turned.

His eyes filled with tears. "No," he said. "Not that. Please." Jim ran down the bank until he reached the field. Tears blurred his vision, but it didn't matter. The barn had fallen over. He ran closer to it, then sat among the weeds of the unused field. The wet ground penetrated his clothing and his body as he sobbed, his face in his hands. He rocked back and forth. "No," he kept repeating. "No, no, no."

When Becky reached him and touched his shoulder, he was still rocking and crying. "I'm sorry," she said. "What can I do?"

Jim looked up. Then he lowered his head once again. "I just wanted you to see it. It's too late."

"There's the house," she said.

"Yes, the house." He looked over at it.

"It's not all lost." She looked exhausted, run down, soaked. Like a rag doll left out in the rain, her arms hung limp and her water-darkened hair stuck to her cheeks and flat against her head.

"It was me," Jim said, "the barn and the house. Part of me is dead. That's it."

"You're not dead. You're alive. This is only old wood, a barn and a house, vacated. You're not vacated or deserted," Becky raised her voice in exasperation.

He wasn't listening. In a moment he got up. "I guess I always hoped I'd beat it. But it's going to happen. There's no stopping it." The barn was his proof.

"You can't give up because of this," Becky said. "It's been here longer than you have, much longer. If it's a symbol of anything, it's how much life you can live if you choose. Are you not choosing?"

"I don't want to die yet. There's more I must do. I wanted us to grow back together, like the old days."

"They're past. We need to build onto today. You forget what we have, what's available to us now."

He thought for a moment. "I should show you the inside of the house, at least. There's love in there. Maybe if you can see the love, touch it somehow…"

Becky took his hand. "Are you sure? What if it's no longer in there, whatever it is you need to show me?"

"It'll be there," he said.

"What if it's not?" Becky persisted.

"Let's go." He got up.

They went into the house together. Jim shook his head to spin off some of the water. Becky patted her hair down and brushed it back with her fingers. She unzipped her jacket. "It's warm in here after that walk."

Jim pulled his coat off and started up the stairs. His eyes were dry, but his face looked tired. He looked much older than he had that morning. He walked slower, more carefully, like a stair might break loose and send him into the basement or backward down into the living room.

Becky followed, apprehensively. Her fear was that whatever

they found would send him into his own thoughts of death, would take him from her permanently. But there was nothing she could do. They had come too far. She followed him into the master bedroom.

He stood near the side of the bed, his hand rubbing the faded quilt, a serene half-smile on his face. "Brad said," he never lifted his eyes from the quilt, "that they must have been in love. That their children couldn't bear to remove it from their bed."

"It's beautiful." She watched him. The window behind him haloed his body with mist and fog, and the out-of-focus green of the hillside trees in the distance. The room was in twilight. He looked so appealing to her she began to cry from the thought of losing him.

Jim looked up. "Your tears. I'm sorry if I hurt you by all this."

Becky reached out and touched the quilt, her fingers lightly sliding over the top of it. Then her hand grabbed it firmly as she bunched it into her fist. Her other hand flew to her mouth. She coughed a sob into it. "We never lost it. I didn't. I can tell you. I've always loved you. We just didn't touch any more. Do you know what it's been like for me these years, not touching? No contact?"

"But when I tried. . ." He couldn't finish.

"You did it out of guilt. You tried. I didn't want you to try; I wanted it to be there. No questions, no guilt."

"What have I done?" he whispered.

When he turned his head up to meet her eyes, she gave a little smile. "You were human. As much as you may not have wanted to be, you were. It took me some time to accept it, but that time is long gone. It has been."

"You've been waiting for me?" he asked, eyes raised.

"No, I've taken what you could give honestly. If it didn't feel honest to me, I rejected it. If it seemed planned or like a weak attempt at something that wasn't you, I rejected it."

"What if it was me? What if that was my way?" he said.

"I'm human too," she countered.

Jim walked around the bed and reached out to her.

Becky fell into his arms and laid her head on his shoulder. Her hair wet his shirt through. They held tight. She sighed. "You're not gone yet. Don't leave me alone before you have to."

Jim put his cheek against her wet hair and rested it there. She had been right. This moment felt true and honest. He could feel it; it was like peace, not anxiety or arousal, but peace. He couldn't have tried to find it, nor could he have planned out its circumstances. It had to happen unsolicited, without thought. He loved her, but he had to forgive himself to do it right. They stood there a long while. When Becky lifted her head, the moment was gone, but the feelings remained.

"I like this place," she said.

"It's important now, isn't it?"

"Yes, but not as important as you are to me. I'm sorry it took this. We should have come here sooner."

"We couldn't. The place was here, but not the time. It wouldn't have worked earlier in time. We are at the right place now, and only now," he said. "It's like everything, we're not ready for it until it happens. But when it happens, we don't always know we're ready."

"Just accept it as it comes," she said.

"More or less."

"And the deer? Why them?" she wanted to know.

"I chose them for some reason. Maybe it was the years of hunting them that made them so important to me. They are on my mind often enough."

"Then they were a figment? Is that what you're saying, now?"

"Not at all. With all my heart, I know they were real, but if I am the gift and the giver, then they are also a part of me."

Becky shook her head. "It's too confusing for me. It almost goes in circles."

"It does, I admit it. But if I am part of everything and I also help to create it, I can be the gift and the giver of the gift. I must be. But I couldn't have done it until I was ready to accept it."

She held him close. "Will I ever see a miracle?"

"Every day you're alive. I believe that."

She kissed him. "We'd better go."

"Can I look at the barn first?"

"Be careful. I don't want to lose you now that you're here."

Jim felt changed. In a moment, it happened. And through a small circumstance. He wondered if Becky was equally overcome with the change, or had she seen it coming, somehow? It was as though he had been walking next to the path for a long time, beating through thickets and hacking at vines. At any moment he could have stepped sideways and been on the path, clear and easy, but he never saw it, never looked. He had been too caught up in his own tortuous progress to look to the side. While Becky followed him the whole way, walking the path, waiting for him to realize it existed. How could he be so smart and so stupid?

He followed Becky downstairs and took her hand once they were outside.

"We'll go together," she said by way of an answer to his unasked question.

He helped her with her jacket, then put on his own. The rain still drizzled in a fine, fog-like mist. A small breeze blew the weeds at an angle, rippling through the field to suggest the movement of some large, fast animal. The current of wind pushed at their backs as they walked toward the crumpled barn.

One wall had collapsed completely into splinters. The rest of the barn had folded one wall into another. In his mind the collapse had occurred like a death dance. The tug of war between gravity and purpose. It saddened him that not a soul had been around when it happened.

As Becky and he got closer to the pile of wood propped up by inside walls still struggling to stand, he ran the collapse over and over again in his mind. The shear size of the wreckage became overwhelming. It became harder for him to visualize the barn's slow demise. More pieces came into view, creating a more complex turn of events, no longer as simple as one wall folding into another. "It's all so complicated," he said.

"Would you want it simple?" she asked.

She was right, he thought. He wouldn't want it to be simple. It was just that the pure complexity of it became overwhelming, much bigger and more powerful than he could contain inside what he considered to be his small and insignificant mind.

He stood near the barn. Becky held back and let him step closer. He remembered how it had been laid out, but little of that could be seen now. Though large sections were still intact, it resembled a pile of wood more than a barn. Jim wanted to cry, but found that he couldn't. He wasn't cried out; it was something more. It was acceptance. The barn was how it was supposed to be. He knew that. There was nothing to mourn, nothing to regret. It looked as natural now as it had when it was standing, maybe more relieved of tension. He wondered, *What does it mean as a symbol, as a key to the rest of the world?* He stepped closer and slipped a little on the wet grass. He heard Becky gasp behind him. "I'm all right," he said. "Just slipped."

"It's okay, Honey," she said.

He stood still for a few more minutes, as his eyes scanned the fallen barn. Its familiar, yet unfamiliar, look gave him that comfortable feeling one gets when a new town becomes familiar.

The rain had soaked the wood to a dark brown punctuated with patches of black. It gave the whole heaping pile a hazy outline. A rising fog hovered over scene, denser in some areas than others. At times the barn looked as much like it was rising from the ground as it did that it had fallen.

When Jim finally turned away, Becky was soaked once again. Looking at her, he felt his own dampness—the uneasy way it reached through his clothes, how it cloaked his head—and decided it was time to return to the heat and dryness of the cabin.

They held hands during the trip back, securing a renewed bond between them. In their silence they were gluing back the missing pieces of their life together, and rummaging through the attics and basements of their memories, collecting only those things of true value.

Chapter 13

The cancer spread. Chemotherapy failed, radiation had been stopped. Jim no longer wanted to fight. He wasn't tired, nor was he ready to die. Instead, he felt it best to fall easily into the flow. Wherever it took him, whatever that meant, he'd accept it not as a sentence, but a choice, a gift in every sense of the word.

One week before his death, nearly a month after their foray to the old farm, and after many long, heartfelt talks and hugging sessions, Jim and Becky joined like they hadn't for many years. Possibly for the first real time in their lives. He no longer needed to blame himself for their separation. Once accepted, rather than worked with or understood, there were no more boundaries. He had to just be.

The evening their connection happened, Jim was sitting in his chair in the living room. The television was off. He watched the occasional lights from passing cars shadow-shift through the room. Becky had gone to bed after they had a long talk. Jim wanted to be awake to experience the night. He let himself feel the air and taste it. He watched the shadows and the light, noticed how the vibrant colors of the curtains, walls, and furniture were struck by the headlights' glow. With the windows partially open, he smelled and felt the breezes push into the house.

The curtains waved, drawing his attention. That's when he saw her shadow out the corner of his eye. She stood near him, naked. When he turned toward her, she spoke.

"I am here for you."

"I know. You always have been." It was a continuation of their earlier conversation, but it had other meanings too. She stepped closer, nervous, slow. Her breasts were like white cups, her nipples dark and hard from the chill night air. Jim stared and she let him. Her stomach was slack and he could remember when it had been firm. *She still has perfect legs,* he thought, *and a smooth, soft butt.* This woman, though, was more than her body. He had always felt that way. It was important that she, too, understood it now.

"You wanted to sit together," she said. She reached out to him. "You said you wanted to look at me that way again."

"Yes." Jim got up from his chair and took her hand. "You look beautiful."

"I'm scared."

"After all these years?"

"Especially. You must remember me when I looked better?"

"Never better than now," he said.

Becky helped Jim strip down and they stood together in the

dark, both as vulnerable at they could be. "I want to look at you too," she finally said. "That's why I'm here."

"The gift and the giver."

"Is it always that way? For each of us?" Becky asked.

"I think so."

"You think too much, sometimes. Maybe we should touch more and think less." Becky led him to the center of the living room. Darkness, and a light glow from the streetlights, fell around them as they sat, cross-legged on the floor, facing one another.

Neither could talk, but both looked at each other's body in the half-light. Jim was first to reach out and touch Becky on the arm, then the knee and up her inner thigh. She explored his neck and shoulders, the fleshy skin near his waist. They leaned to kiss, but soon returned to their touching and staring.

"Turn around," Becky said. "I want to look at your back. I've always loved how your shoulders look under your shirt."

And so it went, touching and exploring until the slow growth of their love overtook them and they coupled, joined, like never before. With their own reasons and agenda, they followed their hearts to the same place at the same time. They loved and fell asleep together on the living room sofa.

One week later, Jim died in the hospital after admitting himself because he felt nauseous. Becky was at work.

The family and close friends met at their house after the graveside ceremony. Brad and Susan stood close by Becky the whole time.

In her mind, Becky relived, over and over again, their last romantic night together. No one knew what she felt, but there was a lightness to her that she couldn't explain… even to herself. He had said he'd be glad to see Connie once again. That he missed her. And Becky was happy for him, now, that he could be with her. They could look after one another.

Brad took Becky's arm and walked her into the kitchen. "Mom, Dad didn't go. He didn't die. He just stepped into another room."

Becky smiled. She understood what he was trying to say and appreciated it. "That sounds just like something your father would say."

"Oops." He smiled shyly, returning her sense of happiness, even though, under the circumstances, it felt odd.

"You're a lot like him." She felt satisfied with that thought. "But I don't want to go from room to room looking for him."

"I didn't mean that, Mom," he began to protest, saw it was unnecessary. "But you're right. You'll need to go on."

"He's everywhere now anyway." Only she knew what she meant. Brad couldn't possibly know what she felt, thought, knew, inside.

"I'm sorry about all the hard times, Mom."

"You misunderstood me, Honey. I want him to be everywhere. I'll miss him for a long time, but he'll be here also." She quietly cried and leaned her head onto Brad's shoulder. She hadn't noticed before, but his back felt just like Jim's. Becky sensed certain happiness for Susan then, and reminded herself to talk to her daughter-in-law about it. Maybe she could give something to Susan, something from herself. *Giving is taking*, she thought. *That's something Jim would have pulled from the idea. But for him it wouldn't have rested there, it would be shifted by his continual need to better understand it. Even if it came around to the same thing in the end, he'd move it through a variety of changes, look at it from all angles.* "I miss him and I'm glad he's gone on," Becky said. She could tell from Brad's face, he had no idea what she meant and didn't know how to respond. "He's safe where he is," she told him as an explanation. "And he's where he should be. Just as we are." She kissed Brad lightly on the forehead.

Susan walked into the kitchen. "I'm sorry, did I interrupt?"

"Not at all," Becky said. "Not at all. You came in at just the right time."

Terry Persun

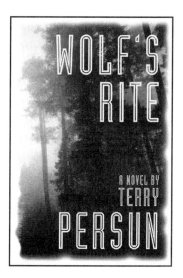

Wolf's Rite

While isolated in the New Mexico wilderness, Llewelyn (Wolf) Smith, an egotistical advertising executive, spends several days fasting while experiencing the rigors of a Native American vision quest.

Forced to fast, Wolf lives for several days inside the borders of a medicine wheel etched into the ground. Inside the ring, Wolf prays to the elements and learns valuable life lessons from a spider, ant, wild dog and hawk.

Upon his return to civilization, Wolf is picked up for the murder of a vagrant Indian found dead near his medicine wheel. A lawyer friend, Gary, must represent Wolf in court. Complicated by the fact that Wolf has slept with Gary's wife, the two must come to terms to remain friends. Wolf must also search his soul for his authentic self, re-establish his place in the business world, and structure his life according to his newfound integrity.

Awards:
Winner: Star of Washington Award
Winner: POW First Place Award for Best Novel
Finalist: ForeWord magazine Book-of-the-Year award

www.TerryPersun.com

Terry Persun

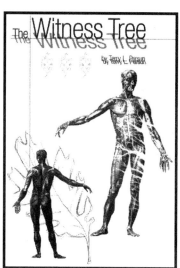

The Witness Tree

Narrated from the point of view of an old oak tree, this novel explores the connection between man and nature.

Lewis begins his life with an unusual connection with the natural world around him through a 'common thought', which provides him with an ability to create the essence of nature in his paintings. Even at a young age, he is extraordinarily perceptive and talented. His twin brother, Jeffrey, on the other hand, is better connected with the business world and eventually takes on the responsibility of selling Lewis' original works.

The stronger Lewis connects with nature, though, the further he gets from what is considered a normal life, which he strongly desires. Yet, as he pushes towards such a life, he loses his connection with common thought and finds himself lost in an uncreative void. Eventually, Lewis must choose between his art and the more normal life he has always longed for.

The Witness Tree is a story of the spiritual journey of one man who is forced to decide his own path in life. This book will engage the reader into rethinking his or her life choices. The ideas explored here will stick with you for a long time.

www.TerryPersun.com

A Word About Our Books

Having worked as an editor for the past 40 some years, I've noticed that the quality of writing being published today is all over the board. I've read some great works and some miserable works. What I've noticed most, though, is that the reader doesn't always know what good writing is. Nor do many of them care. What the reader wants is a good story, reasonably written.

A writer can't experiment if the structures are too stringent, yet they can't be understood if the structures are removed altogether. Balance is what I look for while evaluating the manuscripts that slide over my desk.

The books we choose to publish at Palmland Publishing are eclectic in subject matter, yet all have two things in common: the writing is clear and the stories are interesting.

In my opinion, that's what this business is all about: interesting stories. Read something from our list. If you like it, read another, then tell all your friends and neighbors about us. Tell them there's a new publisher in town who is going to upset the apple cart.

And most of all, enjoy the read.

Robert Fulton Jr.

Robert Fulton, Jr., PhD
Editorial Director

www.PalmlandPublishing.com